HUMAN HARVEST
ALIEN ABDUCTION

ANTHONY GIANGREGORIO
KEITH ADAM LUETHKE

OTHER LIVING DEAD PRESS BOOKS

HUMAN HARVEST: ALIEN ABDUCTION

PROLOGUE

Jake parked his Jeep Cherokee along a lonely stretch of road, where the darkness would hide his desires. He turned to Brittney and put an eager arm around her shoulders. They had been together long enough for his attention to seem complacent.

"Are you sure about this? We don't have to if you're not ready," he said, but his eyes begged differently.

Brittney, two years younger than him, was slender with long, smooth legs. She squeezed his hand and smiled. "I'm positive. I want you to be my first, Jake."

That was all the incentive he needed. He gazed into her dark blue eyes and kissed her deeply. She sucked on his lips and touched his upper thigh.

They kissed for a few moments, happy to be in each other's company. Jake eased his hand up her backside and was about to unhook her bra when a steady beeping came from out of nowhere.

"What's that noise?" Brittney asked, now tense.

Beep. Beep. Beep. Beep.

Jake nibbled on her neck, too occupied to care. "It's just the radio, ignore it."

She pulled away from him. "That's not the radio, Jake. The car isn't even on."

He sighed, breaking their warm embrace. He took the key out of the ignition but the monotone beeping continued.

"That's weird, I don't know what's making that sound," he said.

She glanced out the window and into the night but all she could see was the darkness surrounding them on all sides, pressing in like a vice.

"I'm worried, Jake."

"I know," he said as he slid the key back into the ignition. When the engine didn't turn over, he slammed his fist onto the dashboard in frustration.

Beep. Beep. Beep. Beep.

"Why won't the car start?" she asked, her voice shaking slightly as she grew nervous.

"I don't know. It should be fine. I just had it tuned up last week."

"Jake, please start the car, I want to leave now."

He pumped the gas pedal and twisted the key to no avail.

"Jake, please take me home. I want to go," she pleaded.

"I'm trying, I'm trying."

She was looking back and forth, as if expecting some horror movie monster to appear at any moment, like out of a bad drive-in film, when she gasped at the sight behind the Jeep. "Jake..." she trailed off.

Jake pulled his eyes away from the ignition and his gaze went to the rearview mirror. "Oh, God, what the hell is that?"

A luminous blue light shined down from the sky, pushing back the night, and heading directly towards the parked Jeep. Jake stared at the radiant glow, trying to pierce the white light. Was it a helicopter or a low flying aircraft?

As he stared at the light, he was just able to make out the outline of a triangular-shaped object.

Scared out of her mind, Brittney screamed, the object drawing closer with each beat of the young couple's hearts. She dug her nails into Jake's arm, but he was too shocked to notice until she dug in deep into his flesh and the sudden pain tore him from his stupor.

We've got to get out of here, he repeated over and over in his head.

A voice, not Brittney's, spoke in his mind. *No, stay there, just stay there*, it demanded.

Jake grabbed Brittney's wrist and kicked the driver's door open, pulling her out as the strange craft hovered over the tree line.

A single beam of light stabbed out of the craft and touched down about ten feet away from Jake's Jeep.

As Jake all but dragged Brittney along behind him, she suddenly stopped, frozen in place.

Four figures had appeared on the road, and at first Jake thought they were men.

But as Jake and Brittney watched, they realized they were not men at all, but something else.

"We need to get out of here," Jake said to her. "I don't know who they are and I don't want to know."

But Brittney had become an unmoving statue, for all purposed looking as if she'd been hypnotized. Jake jerked her harder by the arm, desperate to leave this place.

"Run, dammit, run!" he screamed as the humanoid figures advanced. The figures seemed to move as one entity, like water breaking through a dam, their movements fluid.

Jake wrapped an arm around Brittney's waist and hoisted her over his shoulder as if he was a fireman and she was the damsel in distress, and with one last glance over his shoulder at the approaching quartet, he ran for the safety of the nearby woods.

The blue light followed him as he ran, Brittney bouncing on his shoulder, a constant reminder of his fleeting hopes for escape. He had nowhere to run to, nowhere to hide. The forest offered little protection and it was only a matter of time before the strange beings caught up with him.

Jake ran for all he was worth, pumping his legs into the hard November soil and avoiding fallen logs as Brittney lay like a mannequin on his shoulders. Behind him, he could hear the footsteps of his pursuers as they stepped on dry leaves and twigs.

As Jake ran deeper into the woods, his mind raced with what he'd seen.

Who were these figures and what did they want? He wondered if he should just stop and ask them, but as the idea crossed his mind, he knew he would do no such thing.

The way they had appeared and their silence didn't bode well for him or Brittney, so he lowered his head and ran, praying he could find help before they caught him.

Brittney stirred in his arms and he slowed to let her down. Looking behind him, he saw no sign of his pursuers. He could only hope he'd lost them for good.

"What, where are we?" she asked as she realized they were in the middle of nowhere.

"In the woods, about a half mile from my Jeep," he said. "We need to run, Brittney. Those people are still following us."

"People? Wha..." she began and then a blue light cut through the trees to the right of where they stood.

"Come on, they found us," Jake hissed as the young couple darted through the trees.

Branches reached out and slapped Jake's face, Brittney huffing and puffing behind him. But he wouldn't let go of her hand and he all but dragged her like a small child attached to her father as they ran for the last bus of the night.

They were lost, Jake knew that but still he ran; his only hope was to put as much distance between him and his followers.

But each time he thought he and Brittney were safe, the blue light flashed through the trees, cutting off their escape.

For all their efforts, Jake and Brittney couldn't outrun the figures, and as they rounded a large oak tree pockmarked with disease, they stopped in their tracks as the four figures seemed to float ahead of them.

"But how?" Jake gasped as he breathed in a lungful of air. Only seconds ago, the four figures had been behind them.

"I...I can't run anymore, Jake, I'm too tired," Brittney said by his side as the figures moved closer.

Jake wanted to pick her up and carry her, but he was exhausted. His legs ached, his arms were sore, and his back was killing him. His eyes took in the left and right of the shadowed woods and he knew he might be able to make a run for it, but then he would have to leave Brittney behind.

He knew he could never do that to her.

As the figures seemed to hover closer, as if floating on a pillow of air, Jake turned to Brittney and held her tight. "I love you, don't you ever forget that," he said to her as his heart beat a mile a minute.

"I love you, too," she said as she wrapped her arms around him, holding him tightly.

When the figures reached the two young lovers, Jake clutched Brittney and wouldn't let go.

Suddenly he felt his entire body go numb and both he and Brittney fell to the forest floor, but despite this, he used all his willpower to hold onto his young love, protecting her to the last.

But he was no match for the ethereal figures and they picked up Brittney and pulled her away from him. Only his hands on her arms kept him connected to her. He stared in horror as inside the white light, Brittney's legs were severed from her torso, blood shooting out to bathe the nearby trees scarlet. She screamed in agony, calling out his name, but all he could do was hold on to her, tears flowing down his cheeks as he watched her being dissected.

As her torso was spilt in two, and her glistening organs floated in midair, he truly came to grasp with his dire situation, and as Brittney's eyes went blank and her head slumped forward as she hung suspended in the air, he cried out to her, feeling the loss of his love and also for himself. For when they finished with her, they focused their strange instruments on him.

Though he screamed in agony as his chest was split from neck to groin, it wasn't until they severed his arms that he finally released Brittney, and succumbed to their large, black eyes.

CHAPTER ONE

Weston Bradley held his cell phone close to his mouth and whispered, "I'm being followed."

Silence greeted him and for a moment he wondered if the line was dead, but then a feminine voice of concern replied, "Who's following you?" She sounded worried and entertained at the same time.

"Orientals in an old black Buick, at least I think they're Orientals. All of them are wearing sunglasses, but they have slanted eyes."

"And for how long have they been following you?" Catherine Avalon breathed heavily into the phone.

"For about a month now, they've never dared get this close before."

"Where are you now?" she asked.

"I'm outside the book store on Kingston Street," he said.

"So, what do you think they want?"

"I don't know, but I'm going to find out. I'll call you back in a couple of minutes."

Weston hung up before she could protest his actions. He loved Catherine, but she was always asking him too many questions to answers he simply didn't have.

The old Buick with tinted windows was parked near the curb, the engine idling softly. Inside, four men watched him from behind dark sunglasses.

A cold shiver crawled along his spine and made the hairs on the back of his neck stand up straight. Who were these men? Where did they come from? What did they want with him?

He was tired of running away from them. They had been parked across the street from his job at the book store for nearly two weeks now, and once, he had called the police on them, but they drove away before the authorities arrived, as if they knew he had alerted them to their presence.

Deciding to take more affirmative action, he swallowed the lump in his throat and approached the Buick. As he watched them through the front windshield, the men in the vehicle didn't stir, but continued to stare at him through their black lenses.

The passenger window rolled down. When he stopped and looked inside the car, his heart was thumping wildly in his chest for the sight before him had to be some sort of joke. A gag perhaps orchestrated by some of his friends.

The men who he'd taken for Orientals weren't Orientals at all. As they sat in the car, he saw they weren't wearing sunglasses, as they scrutinized him with oval shaped, black eyes the deepest color of outer space and the blackest depths of the ocean.

"Is this some kind of a joke? Why are you following me, what do you want?" he asked.

He waited for a reply, but the man in the front seat didn't have a mouth to speak from. Where lips should part for speech there was only a thin line like that of an unfolded paper clip. Then, the man spoke without moving his lips, Weston seeming to hear the words in his head, as if it was he that was thinking the words.

We're going to core your head out.

Weston backed away from the old Buick as his mouth fell open in shock. He may have stood there forever if he wasn't jarred back to reality when his cell phone began to ring.

"Stay back. Stay away from me," he warned, his right index finger pointing at the four men with weird eyes in an accusing gesture.

A few pedestrians walked by him as he stood near the Buick, either uncaring or too busy to be bothered by a stranger rambling on the sidewalk.

The figure in the car rolled up the window, blocking the interior from view once more.

The Buick's engine roared and the car took off down the street, disappearing around a corner. Weston watched it leave, not knowing then, that from today, his life would forever be changed.

CHAPTER TWO

Catherine slammed her cell phone down on the metal gurney. A small crack appeared on the LCD screen. She didn't mean to break it, but Weston was making her upset again with his foolishness.

Why is he doing this to me?

She sighed and tucked the phone into a pocket in her medical scrubs. She and Weston had only been together for a month, sharing pleasantries, kisses, books they enjoyed, taking things slow.

But after his strange phone call, how could she not question his sanity.

Honestly, people following him...why on earth would they want to? It's not like he's important or anything.

But he was special in her eyes; an avid reader, muscular, and very nice. He had no secrets. He lived alone in a two bedroom apartment and kept to himself.

Why would anyone follow him? Unless he saw something someone didn't want him to see? That's silly, like a bad story from a cheap novel.

Catherine turned her jumbled thoughts off. She was getting sidetracked from work, and couldn't afford to make a mistake because she was thinking about Weston. He was on his own, at least until she finished working on the cadaver before her.

She leered over the corpse on the medical table, shaking her head at the terrible loss of a life so young.

The boy had brown, short-cropped hair, weighed a little over a hundred pounds, and was only thirteen years old. The police report indicated that he'd died from being pushed out of a window, and had suffered a broken neck from the fall. Catherine shook her head at the tragedy and searched for a vein in his jugular. The report also stated the death was an accident. Another boy had playfully shoved him into the glass, it shattered, and he fell to his death.

An accident, yeah, tell that to him.

Catherine found an artery and cut into the boy's neck with her scalpel. She then stuck a metallic tube in to let the blood drain from the body where it would flow down the table and drip into a drain in the floor as she connected another tube on the other side of the neck and pumped in embalming fluid.

She tried to forget what Weston had said, but couldn't seem to stop thinking about their conversation. He was always making her worry in one way or another; sometimes she enjoyed the feeling because it proved to herself that she cared about him. But other times, like today, she hated feeling this way, and needed to talk to him, if only to confirm he was okay.

She checked her cell phone for missed calls, remembered breaking it on the table, and cursed. It was going to be a long day as an embalmer at the funeral home.

* * *

Catherine called Weston three times on the office phone before giving up. Five bodies embalmed and ready for their burials later, she left work for the day. She wanted to drive straight to Weston's apartment, but drove home instead. She hoped he might be there, waiting for her since she had given him his own key a week ago. Even if he wasn't there, it would still be no call for alarm, she promised herself. He could handle his own affairs.

She hopped in her tan colored Volvo and peeled out of Brier Funeral Home. Catherine chewed on her lower lip, nervous about Weston and the strangers he'd mentioned. Weston had first brought them up a few weeks ago.

They were having a picnic in the park, consuming homemade falafels and enjoying each others company when a lanky man in dark glasses came from the woods and sat by the lake, about thirty feet away from them. Weston's gleefulness emptied as he watched the man. Sensing his panic, Catherine had questioned him immediately. Weston told her to be quiet. They watched as the man rose, walked up to them, nodded in greeting, and walked away. Catherine thought the entire scenario was very commonplace and nonchalant. Weston, on the other hand, was paralyzed with fear. He went into a tirade, whispering in her ear about four men who weren't really men but something else. Catherine asked him what kind of medication he was on, and he laughed, telling her he only took a fish oil tablet once a day. They swept the matter aside, left the park, and he never brought it up again until today.

Catherine exhaled as she thought about Weston some more. She'd always had a habit of attracting the wrong type of men. Every time she met a nice guy, he either had an alcohol problem or couldn't seem to function in society or she found out he was married and had lied to her. Her mother told her it was in her nature to be approached by the weird ones, as though the blood running through her veins was a magnet to their kind, but she hoped Weston was different. He had a steady job as the assistant manager of a used book store, a small apartment in a suitable neighborhood, no crazy ex-girlfriends—as far as she knew, and no overbearing parents. He was just a great guy who respected her and took things slow and besides his paranoia about being watched, he was just about perfect.

She made a sharp, right turn and came upon her modest cottage home at the outskirts of town. The three bedrooms, two bathroom home was set far back amongst the trees, offering plenty of quiet and privacy. She'd inherited the place when her parents died ten years ago in a train crash. They bought the house as a place to spend the summer, but after her father, an architect, lost his high-paying job, they'd moved here exclusively, and sold the condo in the city. Catherine had fond memories of living here, and each time she pulled into the driveway, she still expected to see her father chopping firewood and her mother busy in the garden at the side of the house. But now the garden was nothing but weeds and her parents were long gone and would never return. They were allowed a second life only through her faded memories which diminished more each day.

She was surprised to find two police cars and an ambulance in her driveway. When she came to a halt beside one of the police cruisers, a large man in a sheriff's uniform, complete with hat, waved to her and exited his vehicle. Catherine did the same.

"What's going on here, Officer?" she asked, dumbfounded. "This is my house."

The middle-aged and well fed man approached her and said, "Hello, ma'am, I'm Sheriff Debussy. Is this your home?"

"Yes, I just said that," she replied, eager to know what was going on. She spotted two men with dogs probing the back of the house, looking for something.

"There's been an accident near your property."

"What kind of an accident?" she demanded.

Sheriff Debussy wiped his brow with the back of his hand. Though it was cool outside, he was sweating heavily.

"Can we go inside, Miss..."

"Catherine, just call me Catherine. And yes, let me get my things first."

"Of course, take your time," he said, politely.

She emptied her car of a gym bag and cooler; the bag was for her spare clothing, and the cooler held a container of uneaten potato salad she'd decided not to eat at lunch. She put the bag over her shoulder and carried the cooler in her left hand.

"Can I help you carry anything, miss?"

"No thanks, I got it," she replied curtly, and walked him to the front door.

Once inside, she brewed a pot of coffee and ushered the sheriff to the dining room table.

"So, are you going to tell me why your men are patrolling my property or is it a secret?"

Sheriff Debussy, worn and sleep deprived, leaned forward in the chair.

"Mr. Martin, your closest neighbor, reported a luminous, blue light last night in the forest. An officer was dispatched but found nothing. But then one of our patrols found an abandoned Jeep Cherokee about a half mile from here. We ran the plates and discovered this morning that the vehicle belonged to a missing teenager, his girlfriend also missing. I can't give you his name, but he went on a date last night and never came home. His parents became worried and filed a report."

Catherine raised an eyebrow. She did recall witnessing a strange blue light shining through her bedroom window, but figured it was just the moon or those new car headlights with the odd glow.

"So why is there an ambulance outside? Did they find them yet?" she choked.

"Yes," Sheriff Debussy sighed, aging before her very eyes. "They were in the woods about two hundred feet behind your house. Dead, I'm afraid."

Catherine swallowed a lump in her throat.

"Dead...were they...murdered?"

Sheriff Debussy narrowed his eyes at her comment. "Perhaps, but I really can't comment on that part any further. You understand. I will say it's possible it might've been an animal attack, but homicide hasn't finished its investigation yet. Tell me, did you see or hear anything out of the ordinary last night, ma'am?"

She thought back to last night. After talking to Weston, she'd taken a shower and gone to bed. Except for the strange blue glow, nothing had seemed out of place. No cries for help. No pleading. Not even a scream, but then the woods had a habit of absorbing sound which was why she loved it out here.

She cleared her throat and said, "I do recall a bright light coming through my bedroom window, but I was trying to sleep and didn't think much of it at the time."

The sheriff eyed her suspiciously. "You mean you witnessed a luminous blue glow from outside and simply went back to sleep?"

"Yes, well, I was very tired," she insisted. "Besides, it was just a light. What was I supposed to do?"

Sheriff Debussy shifted in his seat. He wanted answers and when he didn't get them his cheeks flushed. "Ma'am, two teenagers are dead. Their families are devastated and this community is going to blame me."

"I'm sorry for you but that's certainly not my problem. I don't know what else to tell you."

He clenched his hands into fists.

"Can I help you with anything else, Sheriff?" she asked. "Or are you through with your questions? I'm tired and want to clean up after work and have my dinner."

Sheriff Debussy sneered and rose from his chair. "No, that's all I have for now, but if I have any other questions I'll call you."

"That will be fine, but as I said, I've told you all I know." She walked him to the front door.

Sheriff Debussy left after telling her a polite "thank you" and she slammed the door behind him and watched from the living room window until the two cruisers, the K-9 Unit, and the ambulance drove away an hour later. Relief flooded through her as the last patrol car vanished around the bend in her driveway.

Finally truly alone, she stripped off her work clothes and slipped into a comfortable pair of shorts and a plain white t-shirt. She was about to eat her leftover potato salad for dinner when the cordless phone in the kitchen rang. She raced to the phone, hoping Weston would be on the other end.

"Hello?" she asked as soon as she picked up the phone and pressed the button to allow her to talk.

If there was someone on the other end of the line, they said nothing.

She pressed the phone closer to her ear and said, "Hello? Is anyone there?"

Then, out of the silence came the strangest voice she'd ever heard; it sounded like someone had gargled shards of broken glass. The voice was unimaginably creepy and somehow voltaic.

"Is this Catherine Avalon?"

"Yes, this is she? May I ask who you are?"

"You don't have much time. Get out the house now before it's too late."

"Excuse me?" Catherine asked, as a sliver of fear coursed down her spine.

"Did you see the blue light last night?" the voice on the other end asked.

"Who is this? If you don't identify yourself I will hang up."

"They're coming for you next. Get out of that house and out of the state. Leave, now."

She wanted to hang up, but something told her to stay on the line.

"I don't know who the hell you think you are, but it's pretty bad when you need to do a prank phone call just for a kick. I can find out who you are, you know, don't call here again, or else," she replied, cutting off the call as she set the phone down.

Though she was trying to be brave, she could feel her heart beating a mile a minute. It was something about the voice, the way it sounded.

Who was that? she asked herself. Her home phone was never the product of prank calls; she knew this because it was an unlisted number. And the person had known her name. She couldn't think of anyone from the past who'd want to scare her. Sure, she'd had her share of bad boyfriends, but what woman didn't?

The phone rang again, making her jump.

Don't answer it, just let it keep ringing, her inner voice instructed, but she picked it up anyway.

"This is my house," she said to herself in a firm tone. "And nobody's gonna threaten me." The words gave her strength as she pressed the *talk* button and said, "Hello?"

"Catherine? It's me, Weston. Are you okay?"

"Weston! Yes, I'm fine," she said with relief. Her dire anger faded away as she spoke. "Where've you been?"

"I'm home. Sorry I didn't call you back right away. I had some trouble."

"What kind of trouble?"

"Those men who were following me... I don't think they're...human."

Catherine laughed as she rolled her eyes. She couldn't help herself. It had been a long day at work, then coming home to the police in her yard, then that bizarre phone call, and now this.

"Look, Weston, I can't deal with this right now," she said. "You're a nice guy and I love spending time with you, but I don't need this in my life right now. I'm too old for games."

Weston was quiet for a moment, the silence seeming to drag on forever.

"I'm sorry you feel that way," he finally said softly.

"Look, it's fine. I've just had a really long day and I need to relax."

"Oh, okay," he replied, realizing she wasn't breaking up with him. "Can I see you tomorrow?"

"Of course you can. I'll stop by the book store around noon. Maybe we can grab lunch."

"That sounds great; noon's fine."

"Good, I'll see you there, goodnight," she said.

"Goodnight."

She hung up the phone and took a wine glass from the cupboard. Weston was kind and understanding, she hoped he stuck around, even with his wild fantasies. She just didn't want to deal with them tonight. Tomorrow, after a good night's sleep, well, one day at a time, right? At twenty-six, she was tired of all the dating and flirting and men coming and going, and she had to admit it was nice to have someone steady for a change.

She poured a red merlot into her glass and stared out the kitchen window, into the night. Two teenagers were killed out there not too far away and she hadn't heard a thing. How was that even possible?

She double checked the locks on the doors and windows before going to sleep, that prank phone call getting to her though she was loathe to admit it. Yet, as she curled under the blankets, sleep never came.

Though she tossed and turned, trying her best to will herself to sleep, she ended up spending the night staring out her bedroom window, praying the blue light she'd witnessed the previous night wouldn't return.

CHAPTER THREE

Weston sat in his recliner, reading an old horror novel that had been on his list of books for ages, before going to bed. He made a promise to himself to read at least ten pages a day no matter what, and he meant to stick to it. He was a few pages away from reaching his goal when the exhaustion caught up to him and he drifted off to sleep.

He was never one to have outlandish dreams. As a child he was prone to dreaming about flying out the window and over town like Peter Pan. His nightmares were far and in between, never anything recurring, and had disappeared as he grew older. But tonight, his nightmares were awakened, haunting him well into the morning.

He dreamed he was a boy again, around ten years old, and in his bed back home. His parents were sleeping in the bedroom down the hall and the house was still and dark.

Weston felt something in the room with him; not his mother checking on him, but something hideous. He watched the door to his bedroom slowly creak open and he attempted to scream but no words came out. He was paralyzed with fear.

A tall, dark figure, slipped inside his bedroom like a shadow creeping along the sidewalk. Beads of sweat poured from Weston's armpits as he watched the shape take form.

It was very tall and slender, graceful, yet cautious. The figure reminded him how he felt around the doctor when they would check his privates and ask him to cough. But the thing before him seemed like it wouldn't bother asking, it would take him and do what it wished.

A name suddenly formed in his head, as if an unknown voice had placed it there. The Watcher.

Weston tried to close his eyes to its presence, but his lids wouldn't move.

The Watcher was still as it studied Weston, observing his frantic behavior, scrutinizing his emotions the way a scientist studied a bug trapped under a microscope.

The staring went on and on. The Watcher was speaking to him in an arcane language, explaining things with its large, black eyes.

Weston's heart was racing, pumping faster and faster until it threatened to explode in his chest. Then, the shape lurched forward, snatching him from his bed, his home, and taking him away into the dark.

Weston jerked out of his recliner in a panic as sweat covered him from head to toe. His book fell on the rug and he lost his page.

"A dream...it was just a dream," he sighed to himself.

Drenched in sweat and still shaking, he went to the bathroom and washed his face with cold water, changing his clothing as well. The nightmare confused him. He tried to reason that the tall figure in his dream was just his mother checking in on him, and that he had let his imagination get the better of him. Maybe his mind was under too much stress lately and this was how it was coping?

Yeah, having a strange man with freaky eyes tell you he was going to core your head out is a good cause for a bad dream. Especially when the words were put into your head.

He wiped his face with a towel and noticed something on the mirror's surface as the steam from the faucet added condensation to the mirror.

When he flicked the bathroom light on, he was shocked to see a four-fingered, no thumb, hand print smudged on it. The fingers seemed separate of themselves and long, much too long for anything human.

His mind began to race with thoughts he'd rather not have.

They were here.

He remembered using the bathroom when he got home, but didn't recall the elongated smudge on the mirror.

The mark was recent and had been placed there while he was sleeping.

A sudden metallic clang erupted from the kitchen and he choked. It sounded like a heavy soup pot had struck the floor. He reeled in on the noise and waited.

Nothing else came from the kitchen.

He gathered his senses and slowly eased into his bedroom. Behind the door was a baseball bat he kept in case of an intruder. The bat was made from oak and heavy enough to fracture a skull. He held the bat in two hands and stalked out of the room. Whoever or whatever had entered his apartment was in for a big surprise.

The floor creaked in the kitchen, followed by a low monotone hum.

This is it, he told himself. *It's time to show them who they were dealing with.*

Weston took a deep breath and launched himself into the kitchen, swinging at empty air.

"Huh?"

The kitchen was empty, but some of his cupboards were open. He quickly checked the rest of his apartment to find it devoid of intruders, and when he had reached the front door, he found it was open. Whoever had violated his home had vanished.

He ran outside, searching for the old Buick, expecting to see it speeding down the road, yet found nothing. The neighborhood was peaceful, everyone sleeping. With the exception of the occasional dog barking in a backyard as it begged to be let in, everything was as it should be.

"I can't believe this is happening," he muttered to himself, then realizing how he must look as he stood on the sidewalk while holding a baseball bat, he went back inside.

After locking his front door, he sat in the kitchen until dawn, waiting for the intruder to try sneaking in a second time.

But as the sun touched the horizon, there was no repeat of the previous night, and the morning's rays found Weston asleep at the table.

This time he didn't dream.

CHAPTER FOUR

Catherine finished her third cup of coffee as she waited outside the book store in her car. Her morning was spent eating a hasty breakfast of black coffee, two pieces of toast, and trying to stay awake. Last night was one of the worst in her entire life. She had feigned sleep in an attempt to fool her body into slumber, but it didn't work. The night was spent staring out her bedroom window into the forest and wondering what had happened to those two teenagers.

The fact that they were murdered so close to her house was unsettling. She wondered who they were and what they were doing out there. Her property was isolated, the nearest neighbor a good mile away. She wracked her brain for answers and could only reach one suitable conclusion: they were seeking a little private time when someone had hunted them down and killed them.

But who would do such a thing?

She wanted to imagine it was a criminal who had escaped from a mental institution, but in her heart she knew that wasn't true. The answer was in the strange blue light, and the possibility that there would be more.

Were their flashlights tinted blue? She had no clue, but hoped they weren't lingering around her property looking for more victims.

Oh, God, she thought. *What will Weston think of me now when I tell him what I'm thinking?*

She'd given him a stern talk about his paranoia, and now she was feeling the same way he did. How could she live that down? She made up her mind then and there not to tell him about the blue light, or the strange phone call, but he did need to know about the double homicide, if he hadn't already heard about it.

The clock on the dashboard reached noon which would mean Weston would get off for lunch now. Like before, he would walk out of the book store wearing a slight frown until he spotted her, and then a smile would spread across his face. She imagined him sweeping her up in his powerful arms and whispering about going back to his apartment for a quick, passionate romp; something they hadn't reached yet in their relationship.

Her day dream popped when Weston exited the store. He wore heavy bags under his eyes and walked like one of the living dead.

Catherine stepped out of her car to greet him. "Hey, honey," she waved.

Weston shuffled over and gave her a faint grin.

"Hi," he said. "I'm glad you came."

She wrapped herself around him, enjoying the closeness of his body. "Me too," she said.

They held each other close and kissed. Her heart fluttered as she moaned into his mouth.

"Wow, you seem cheery today," he said with a grin.

"I'm not, really."

Weston parted from their embrace. "Why, what's wrong?"

"Let's talk about it over lunch," she said. "My treat."

"Okay," he said and took her hand.

They strolled to a take out Mexican restaurant, ordering two taco salads, and eating them outside. Catherine commented on the nice weather, her new high- heels, and avoided the central topic she wanted to discuss altogether. She couldn't bring herself to tell him about the strange events from yesterday and he didn't seem to really want to pry it from her.

Once they finished lunch, they returned to her car and she kissed him goodbye.

"Wait," he insisted. "Didn't you have something to tell me?"

Catherine nodded. "Oh, yes, I guess I did."

"Is it something really bad?"

She shrugged. "It's not really bad, just odd." She paused, noticing an old Buick had slowly pulled up to the curb behind where they stood. Inside were four men wearing dark sunglasses, hats, and trench coats.

Weston gasped when he spotted the car. He grabbed her around the waist and hustled her away.

"What's going on?" Catherine gasped.

"Just keep walking and don't look back."

But even the frantic trembling in Weston's voice wasn't enough to stop her curiosity. She did look back to see that the Buick was now following them.

Catherine came to a sudden halt. "Who are these people, Weston?"

"I...I don't know," he stuttered, watching the vehicle stop again.

"What the hell do they want with you?"

"To core my head out," he replied automatically. "That's what they told me yesterday."

Catherine balled her hands into fists. "That's ridiculous and I'm putting a stop to this right now. They're nothing but a bunch of bullies." She stormed over to the Buick, determined to end this senseless conflict once and for all.

"Hey, you in the car, I want to have a word with you," she called out to them.

"Catherine, don't do this," Weston pleaded. He chased after her, but didn't manage to reach her before she was at the Buick. With nothing else to do, he paused and waited.

The tinted side window rolled down and Catherine shook her finger at the man in the dark sunglasses.

"You've got some nerve..."

Her voice drifted off into silence as she observed the four men in the car a little better. She saw the sunglasses weren't glasses at all, they were big black eyes. They weren't men. They were something else—something bad. Before she had time to react, elongated fingers shot from the window and curled around her arm.

"Catherine!" Weston cried out.

The passenger door was opened and she was dragged into the Buick. But the humanoids inside could only get her halfway inside, as Catherine braced herself at the door frame.

"Get off of me," she demanded.

Then, Weston was there. He managed to curl his arms around her waist and yank her free. Catherine screamed as the Buick's engine roared once and the driver eased off the brake pedal. The car sped down the road, Catherine hanging out the open door, and Weston holding on for dear life. He matched glares with one of the four humanoids inside. Though its eyes were concealed behind dark sunglasses, he could sense a deep hatred generating from them.

He let go of Catherine briefly and reached for one of the dark men. The figure was so obsessed with getting her into the car that it didn't bother to defend itself. Weston raked his nails along its face, scratching the large, opaque eyes in the process. The being shrieked, the yell filling his mind, but it didn't move its slit for a mouth; its hold on Catherine lessened.

Weston punched another one in the face, his knuckles sinking into something he could only equate to reptilian flesh. Once the two humanoids in the backseat let go of her, Weston pulled on Catherine with all his might. They both fell backwards, entangling themselves together, as they both slammed onto the road.

Car horns blared, and a few vehicles nearly crushed the couple, but Weston ignored them, his sole purpose to protect Catherine. He dragged her out of the road, using every last ounce of strength left in him. Once they were on the sidewalk, she embraced him. She trembled in his arms like a newborn brought in from the cold, and he held her tight, trying not to shake himself.

In the distance, he saw the Buick run a red light and speed around the next corner, a few cars screeching their brakes so as not to hit it.

He thought he heard an ominous voice telling him they would return, but he prayed it was only his imagination.

CHAPTER FIVE

"We have to do this," Catherine pressed.

"But nobody will believe us," Weston sighed. "I've already tried this before. Hell, you didn't till you saw them for yourself."

They stood outside the Knoxville Police Department, holding hands and scared out of their wits.

Catherine crushed his fingers as she let out a heavy sigh. "They'll believe us, I know they will. Just let me do the talking and don't mention anything about...their eyes."

"Fine," he nodded.

Catherine entered the building first and was greeted by two police officers and a metal detector.

One man, tall and black with wide shoulders, waved Catherine over.

His voice was a deep baritone as he said, "Please empty your pockets and step through the detector."

Catherine gave him her purse and walked through the detector without a problem.

"Next," the other officer said, a small but strong female.

Weston put his keys and wallet into a small plastic basket and went through the metal detector.

Beep! Beep! Beep! Beep!

The metal detector's whining pulsed in his eardrums like a ban-shee's scream.

"Step over here, sir," insisted the officer. He waved a hand-held detector over Weston's shoes, pants, shirt, and head. When the detector glazed over his head, it beeped loudly.

"Do you have anything in your hair, sir?"

"My hair, well no," Weston answered, running his fingers along his scalp. The officer frowned and brought the detector to the right side of Weston's head and it beeped once more.

"I don't understand this," Weston laughed. "Do you think I have a metal plate in my head or something?"

The officer was firm in his response. "I can't allow you through if I don't know what's beeping, it's policy."

"Hold on a minute," Catherine said. She put her hands on her hips, meaning business. "He's with me."

"I'm sorry, ma'am," snapped the female officer. "He'll have to wait outside if we can't identify the source."

"But..." Catherine hesitated.

"That's okay," Weston said. "I'll wait by the front door. Appar-ently, I have metal in my frigging brain."

Catherine scoffed, about to argue when Weston turned left. She huffed and headed towards the main desk to check in and report her attempted kidnapping.

* * *

Weston leaned against the building and closed his eyes for a moment.

How can this be happening? What do I have in my head?

He thought back to yesterday and what one of the beings in the Buick had said, about how they were going to core out his head.

That chilly, monotone voice made the hairs on the back of his neck stand up.

Did they put something in my head?

He couldn't remember the dark men ever touching him, unless today counted when he planted his fist into one of their faces. His hand was still jarred from throwing that punch, and the feel of...of reptilian skin.

He took a few deep breaths and tried to focus on something else, anything else. He listened to the sounds of a woman walking by in high heels, people laughing nearby, and the noise of the traffic.

They could still be out there, waiting for me.

He opened his eyes and scanned the vehicles roaring past him: a red truck, cream Escort, and a squad car. He breathed a little easier.

They might still be around, but if so, then they're staying out of sight.

Weston crossed his arms as he relaxed a little more. The trip to the police station was a complete waste of time. He was positive that Catherine would storm outside any second now, ranting about how they didn't take her seriously. But the longer he waited, the more his morale improved. She must've been giving them hell in there and knowing her she might even get them to believe her.

He chuckled to himself.

An elderly woman with her grandson walked by and stared briefly, both looking worried about something. He smiled at them as they went by and overheard the boy try to whisper to the old lady, but failing miserably.

"Hurry up, Granny. I don't want the bad man to catch up to us." He gazed over his shoulder and shuffled his feet. The grandmother said nothing, only urged him forward until the two disappeared around the corner.

Weston examined the area the boy was worried about; it was a dark alley. He saw a couple of tall trash cans in the shadows, and figured the boy had a vivid imagination. It was as he continued staring, that one of the trash cans moved. He went perfectly still, motionless, struck by fear as a tall figure in a brim hat, trench coat, and dark sunglasses peeled away from the darkness and moved toward him.

It's one of them. Get out of here, now! a voice yelled in his head.

Weston debated running back into the police department and telling the officers that one of the things stalking him was outside, but before he could move, the dark figure was next to him. It stood a good seven feet tall, stood three feet away from him, and stared at him with eyes lost in the fathoms of space and time.

"Who are you? What do you want from me?" Weston whispered.

An image formed in Weston's head of a thousand stars twinkling from behind a black canopy. They weren't his thoughts, but were coming from the dark figure. In an instant, the stars shifted and jolted forward, lights flashed, and he felt like he was onboard a spaceship as it entered warp speed. Solar systems flashed by, planets made of ice, rock, gas, lava, and water soared through his mind. Then space altered and he was looking at Earth in the same way an interstellar visitor might see it from an orbiting spacecraft. Earth was a small water planet in the middle of a dead solar system.

The dark figure reached for Weston's hand and he broke the spell and leaped backward, avoiding the mysterious figure.

"Get the hell away from me," he rasped. "Whatever you are."

He swung where the dark figure's stomach would be and connected, and it was akin to punching a sack of water, his fist sinking in and then popping back out.

The dark figure flooded his mind with images of television programs. *Leave it to Beaver* played for a few seconds: Wally giving the Beaver advice on how to deal with bullies. Other images came from pop culture, the Hobbits in the *Lord of the Rings* trilogy, the boy from *Where the Wild Things Are* as he befriended the monsters, next an image of Catherine lying naked before him.

"Stop it, stop it now!" Weston cried out, and planted his palms onto the dark figure's chest, shoving hard.

The figure wobbled backward, its dark sunglasses tipping slightly.

Weston paused when he noticed the eyes looking back at him weren't solid black like the others, these were solid blue like the sky on a clear day or the ocean off the French coast.

The dark figure seemed to sense this knowledge and more.

A deep baritone voice broke off their contact.

"Is there a problem here, sir?" a police officer asked, having seen Weston shove the taller figure.

"I...no, no problem," Weston trembled. He turned to face the dark figure, but it was gone. Weston shook his head in disbelief.

"You can come inside now, sir," instructed the officer. He was a little put off by the sudden disappearance of the other figure that had been with Weston a second ago, but said nothing about it. "Your girlfriend's waiting for you."

Weston ignored him, peering into the alley, and wondered if the dark figure was in the shadows somewhere.

"Did you see where that...man...went?" he asked the officer.

The cop gave a vacant stare and replied, "What man?"

"The tall...man I was with. He was standing right here...oh, never mind." Weston pushed beyond the stupefied policeman and went into the building.

Catherine was waiting for him near the metal detector and he stopped before going through it, waving her to him.

"Weston, are you okay?" she asked, seeing the flustered look in his eyes.

"Yeah, I guess so. I saw one of them while I was waiting for you. He was in the alley. He disappeared when that cop came to get me." He shook his head. "But it was like the cop didn't even see it."

"Oh my God, what do they want from you?" she asked, hugging him tightly.

"I don't know, but he wasn't one of the ones that were in the Buick, I know that for sure; he was something else. And he felt, familiar, like I've seen him before."

Catherine trembled in his arms and said, "I filed a police report and described the men in the Buick. I told them how they tried to kidnap me. They said to call if we see them again."

Weston gently brushed a few errant strands of hair off her face. He wanted to kiss her, hold her close, and tell her everything was fine, that they were safe, and nobody would ever touch her again. But the words slipped away before he could speak them, his mind focusing on only one thing.

"Did you tell them they weren't...people?"

Catherine shook her head. "No, of course not," she laughed. "They would think I was insane if I did."

He laughed with her. "Maybe we are," he said, and walked her out of the police building. "But what if it's all true?"

She looked at him as they stepped out onto the sidewalk, seeing the cars buzz past and people going about their business.

"It can't be real, Weston, you know that as well as I do. There has to be a rational explanation for everything that's happened."

"But what if there isn't one?" he prodded.

"Then that would only leave the impossible."

CHAPTER SIX

Catherine suggested they go to her house and Weston complied. He didn't feel comfortable in his apartment, not after the incident this morning.

The late afternoon sunlight was burning through the trees when they reached Catherine's quaint country home. She instinctively searched the surrounding forest upon their arrival for any strangers, but only found a squirrel harvesting nuts for the winter.

Weston waited for her by the car as she walked around her property and upon returning, he climbed out, not understanding what she was doing.

"Is everything okay?" he asked.

Catherine frowned. Everything was not 'okay' and he knew it as well as she did. She gave him a kiss on the cheek as she reached into her pocket for her keys, her eyes playing over the front of her home, checking windows and the front door. Her house was unaltered from this morning. The welcome mat was in the same place, the cat statue on the front porch greeting her as it always did, and there wasn't a living soul in sight. It was as though the double murder in the woods had never happened, and everything was back to normal.

Yeah, except the people in the Buick and that strange blue light that had shined through my window in the middle of the night, everything is just great.

She giggled to herself in disbelief at all the craziness she'd suffered through within the past forty-eight hours. It was all like a bad horror movie and she was the 'B' actress cast to star in the film. But if that was so, then Weston was her leading man and that wasn't so bad.

As if he sensed her uneasiness, he put his hand on her shoulder, trying to comfort her.

"I'm fine," she lied, and walked to her front door, while Weston followed, not saying a word. She unlocked the door and began to step through, but then hesitated in the doorway, stiff and uneasy, a high-pitched scream escaping from her lips.

"What is it?" Weston yelled as he shoved past her, baring his fists at any intruders who dared to break into her home. But there was nobody there, only a long brim hat and a trench coat lying on the rug beside a pair of dark sunglasses.

"They were here. They were in my house," Catherine sobbed, going into hysterics.

"Get a hold of yourself," Weston said as he turned and grabbed her. "I need you to stay focused while we sort this out."

She shrugged free of him and trampled over the familiar garments as she raced for the kitchen.

"Catherine, get back here! They might still be here!"

She returned a second later holding two, large kitchen knives.

"Here, take one," she said, forcing the knife into his hands. "We'll search the house and make sure it's empty."

Weston nodded and stepped in front of her, taking the lead. "All right, but stay close to me."

The house was silent, like a tomb, like death.

Weston eased into the dining room first, poised to thrust at anything with the sharp blade. He walked around the oak dining table, careful not to bump into the high-backed chairs. Catherine stuck close beside him and pointed her knife at every dark shadow. The dining room was empty and he moved onto the bedrooms and then the two bathrooms. He crept down the hallway silently, barely making so much as a sound. He peeked into the first bathroom and then pushed back the shower curtain, but discovered nothing amiss. He pressed onward, while Catherine held onto his shirt tail like a scare child.

This can't be happening. What could they possibly want from me? I'm just an embalmer! she yelled in her head.

She whimpered softly, the stress of the last two days catching up to her.

"You're safe with me," Weston whispered. "I won't let anything happen to you. Just stay close and don't let go of me."

Oh, believe me, I won't, Catherine thought. She braced herself against him, pressing her breasts against his back.

When they reached the first bedroom, which Catherine had converted into an office, she breathed a little easier. The room was the same as she'd left it, nothing out of place or missing, even the few papers she had left on the desk in the same spot; not so much as a breeze had been in here since she had left.

Then, a sound came from her bedroom, loud like a cannon had gone off in the still house—the door slamming closed.

Her back stiffened as the bang echoed through the house.

Oh, God, they're in my room! What're they doing in there?

Weston didn't flinch or pause. He held her hand and ran to the bedroom, the knife leading the way. "Come out of there and face me, you son-of-a-bitch!" he yelled.

The roar in Weston's voice put Catherine's nerves on edge. She'd never heard him yell like that and hoped he wouldn't do it again. She had now changed her mind about searching the house. Now she wanted to run, get in her car and drive away, as fast and as far as possible.

Weston tried the doorknob to the bedroom but it was locked. He reared back to kick the door in but Catherine stopped him. She held up a finger, gesturing for him to wait. She went to a small table at the end of the hall and a second later, she returned holding a thin sliver of metal in her hand. She slid it into the keyhole below the doorknob. A few seconds later, she had the lock picked and slipped the metal into her back pocket.

"It's just a piece of a coat hangar I keep around in case I lock one of the doors by accident," she explained.

"Good job," he said as he got in front of her. He reached down and turned the doorknob, and as it opened slightly, he pushed it open all the way and sliced the air with the kitchen knife as he charged into the room. His eyes went left and right but the bedroom was vacant, except for an open window. The curtains blew back and forth as a gentle wind filled the room.

Weston and Catherine moved toward the window and peered outside, hearing footsteps crunching dead leaves as someone tried to make their escape.

"You better run, you bastard!" Weston called out the window. "I'll kill you if I catch you!"

The footsteps became softer until they vanished, lost in the forest.

Catherine placed her knife on the nightstand, sat on her bed, and buried her head in her hands as she softly wept. Seeing the danger was passed, Weston went and sat down beside her, setting his knife down on the bed.

He hugged her, whispering comforting words into her ear, though both knew that the nightmare they now found themselves in was far from over.

* * *

"You go and take all the canned food out of the kitchen cabinets and I'll pack my clothes," Catherine said as she dragged two luggage bags out from under her bed and started tossing clothes into it. "I'll not stay in this house for a second longer than I have to. Not until this is all over, whatever *this* is."

Weston was a little shocked by the sudden change in her behavior. After she collapsed on the mattress and cried for a good ten minutes, she stood up, closed and locked all the windows, then began packing.

And now we're apparently going somewhere, he thought.

She was busy forcing in pants ands shirts, grabbing her brushes and a makeup kit from her side table. She paused when she saw Weston staring at her, standing still. "What are you waiting for? We have to hurry," she said quickly.

"Catherine, where are we going to go?"

"Don't worry about that, I have a plan," she said as she shoved in clean underwear, taking all of them out of the drawer in one large armful. "Just get all the supplies you can, please."

Weston shrugged and left the bedroom. He knew better than to argue with her. This was her house, after all, and if she wanted to leave then it was fine with him. The refrigerator was all but empty, only a half gallon of milk about to expire, and a few questionable eggs. Weston decided to stick with the canned goods. He found her cupboards overflowing with dry cereals, corn muffin mix, a variety of soups, vegetables, and a stockpile of green tea. As he tossed the cans into the luggage bag in no particular order, the phone rang. He wrapped his hand around the receiver, but stopped himself before answering. He then let it go and took a step back, letting it ring until the answering machine picked up.

Catherine's voice came on the recorder, *Please leave your message after the beep, thank you.*

A terrible shriek like none he'd ever heard before deafened the room. He could only relate the sound to the high-pitched wail of a child when it didn't get what it wanted. He ran to the answering machine and pressed the button, disconnecting the call. The horrible sound was cut off immediately. He rubbed his ears but they continued to ring.

"What the hell was that?" Catherine yelled as she rushed in from the bedroom with two heavy luggage bags under her arms. Her eyes were wide in panic from when she heard the shriek.

"I don't know, but if you have a place in mind we'd better get there fast. We might be having more company," he said.

Her face was firm, her resolve unwavering as she said, "I'm done, let's go."

Weston grabbed one of the bags from under her arms, gathered the canned goods from the kitchen, and followed her outside. She locked the door behind them and looked to Weston. "Seems silly locking the door when I know they can get in whenever they want." She went to her car and opened the trunk for him. "Toss the bags in here and I'll start the car."

Weston flung the bags into the trunk and slammed it closed. Out of the corner of his eye, he saw a brief flash of blue light coming from the forest, but when he tried to get a better look, it was gone. He wondered if he'd imagined it.

Catherine beeped the horn as she started the engine, then slid over for him to drive. "Let's go, Weston."

He saw her sitting in the passenger seat, so he slid behind the steering wheel. When he looked at Catherine for guidance, he saw her lower lip tremble. Though remaining strong, she was on the verge of breaking apart; the only thing holding her together the man at her side.

"Drive out to I-40 East," she instructed.

He glanced at the rearview mirror and witnessed the strange blue glow coming from the forest as it slowly approached the house. He backed up the car, swung it around in a three point turn, then stepped on the gas pedal, speeding down the road and leaving the blue light behind.

Six minutes later, once they were on the highway, he glanced at her and asked, "So where are we going? What's this plan of yours?"

"My parents have a log cabin up in the Smoky Mountains. We'll be safer there, no one knows about it."

Weston nodded, as he focused on the road ahead. The highway was busy as usual, cars and trucks speeding along to points unknown.

Every now and then he'd checked on Catherine to make sure she was all right. In time, as the steady purring of the car lulled her, she leaned back in her seat and closed her eyes, falling into an uneasy sleep.

* * *

Catherine dreamed she was lying on her bed in her home once more. It was dark. It was a peaceful night, but she felt watched, observed. She hid under her thick blanket, as sweat began to drip down her arms and soak into the sheets.

A blue light shone through the bedroom window, as though someone had flicked on a light switch. She tried to get out of bed, but her limbs were frozen; it was like she was paralyzed. Her primal mind was screaming for her to flee, but her body was immobile and wouldn't obey.

Suddenly, the blue light expanded, spreading to all four corners of the bedroom and banishing the darkness.

She gave a silent scream as the bedroom door creaked open. Her breathing came in quick gasps and she felt herself shaking as goosebumps appeared on her arms and legs.

Four figures, tall and thin, drifted into the room through the doorway. They stared at her with big, black eyes and all she could think about was how these things moved like bugs.

But they weren't bugs, they were something much more. They lifted her off the bed without touching her and she floated out the window, becoming one with the blue light. She was so scared, and her heart was beating so fast she thought it might very well explode.

Then the forest was gone and she was in some sort of metallic room. The blue light remained and it reflected off every surface, blinding her.

The figures were by her side then, and they maneuvered her floating body onto a table, no, not a table, an organic device.

"No," she whimpered. "Please don't do this, please."

Four sets of black abyss eyes glared down at her without mercy.

"Obey," said one figure.

"Do as we say," another chimed in. But the words were in her head, as if she had thought them herself.

Catherine couldn't ignore the voices and with her body still paralyzed, she lay prone on the organic table. Though in a total state of fear, she still wondered how she got here. One minute she was flying through the window and the next...

One of the tall humanoids waved a long serrated blade over her.

"Oh, God, please stop this nightmare," she pleaded.

The dark humanoid cut into her flesh without remorse, trading smooth skin for red tendons and shards of bone.

Catherine screamed loud as it showed her bits of herself, each slice of the knife like living fire.

Then, just as soon as it happened, the ordeal was over. The figures lifted her over a circular chamber and below her the floor twisted and morphed like milk poured into a cup of coffee.

When Catherine touched the floor, it opened out into the night. She was falling, fast, the wind blowing her hair about her head as if she was in a wind tunnel. The sensation made her sick and she wondered if she would vomit.

She looked upwards into the night sky, but instead of seeing stars, she saw a massive craft of solid black with red lights along the side.

Below her was a rippling lake, and before she could cry out, she found herself entering the icy water, the leftover blood and tissue of her mangled body floating into the dark waters as she sank below its murky surface.

I'm going to die. Please, wake up. I have to be dreaming. Wake up!

But she couldn't break the spell of the horrible nightmare, and began to choke on the cold water entering her lungs.

Next came the worst thing imaginable: the blue light returned, surrounding her body, encasing it. She closed her eyes tight, willing the light to go away with her mind. A strong force pressed down on her and she sank deep into the lake. The speed at which she was traveling was like being on a roller coaster, only this wasn't a fun ride, this was pure hell. As the blue glow pushed her deeper into the water, her lungs filled and she couldn't breathe. She thrashed, fighting for air and life. The light gave her no mercy; it sensed her struggles and sent her even deeper into the blackness. Her lungs exploded, popping like twin balloons in her chest. She cried out one last time, knowing this would be the end.

She was going to die!

CHAPTER SEVEN

"Catherine, wake up," Weston urged.

She gasped for air then sat up straight in her seat as she put her right hand on her chest, feeling her heart jack hammering.

"Sorry to wake you but I was beginning to get worried," Weston told her.

She let out a deep breath, thankful to be alive, her dream still vivid in her mind. She looked at her arms and touched the skin, as if she expected to see it peeled and shredded, the gleam of white bone peering through the layers of muscle.

"What was...I...I was having a nightmare I think."

"Yeah, well, that must've been one hell of a nightmare."

"I'm sorry," she apologized, replaying the terror she endured in her head.

What did it mean? Did the event actually happen or was it just a nightmare? she wondered.

She remembered the blue light shining into her bedroom window, but didn't remember anyone taking her away. The dream seemed real enough, but she couldn't help thinking she might've been watching the death of someone else.

Weston broke her chain of thought as he shifted lanes and touched her arm gently.

"We're on the highway heading towards the mountains and I needed to know where to go soon."

"Uh, yeah," Catherine replied, sluggish from sleep. She rubbed her forehead, willing the images of the nightmare to fade.

"What's wrong?" he asked, the concern prevalent in his voice. "You feeling sick?"

"No," she answered. "I'm fine. Look for Exit 217 and I'll guide you from there."

Weston's stomach grumbled as he rubbed his belly and made a slight grimace.

"Are you hungry?" she asked.

"Yeah," he grinned as he patted his stomach. "Do you mind if we stop somewhere for a bite to eat?"

"Not at all." She stared out the window into the dark sky.

Weston continued driving.

"What do you think they are?" she asked him. He swerved into the right lane after signaling and slowed down.

Catherine didn't think he'd heard her and was about to ask again when he replied, "Have you ever heard of the *visitors*?"

"No, I can't say that I have."

"I read a book a long time ago called *Intruders* by Budd Hopkins and it was a supposedly true account of a woman being abducted by aliens." He waited for her to laugh but she was speechless.

He continued. "They came to her at night and carried her away into a spaceship so they could perform all sorts of tests on her, kind of like what our scientists do to the animals they study here on Earth."

"What did they look like?" Catherine asked, guessing what he was going to say but wanting to hear it from him.

"They were tall, grey skinned humanoids, and had big, black eyes."

Catherine gulped despite herself. "Do you think those are the same ones we saw?"

"No, it's not them," Weston responded, curtly. "The beings following us have similar eyes but act differently, and drive a Buick, not a spaceship for Christ's sake."

"How do you know for sure?" She hugged herself, feeling a sudden chill. "Maybe they have one stored somewhere, maybe it's in the woods."

"Well, from what I've read, they don't talk to people for one thing or wear trench coats. The aliens from the book kidnap people, perform experiments, and then send them back."

Catherine let out a gasp as a wild thought struck her.

"What is it?" he asked.

"What if this is a new type of experiment? Maybe they learned all they could from abductions so now they're doing something else."

Weston sighed. "I don't know, I just don't know. We have no idea why they're chasing us, what they want, or who they even are. And they almost...took you today."

A tingle spread across the back of Catherine's neck. She leaned over and cuddled beside her man, more for herself than for him.

"But they didn't take me, Weston. You saved me and I'm grateful."

He put his arm around her as he took the exit she indicated. He said nothing until he stopped at a Waffle House located a mile from the exit.

"We're here," he said, and put his fingers through her hair.

She enjoyed the sensation and moaned. "Do we have to stop for dinner? The cabin is only an hour or so away. I could make you something to eat when we get there."

He caressed her back. "I just need to rest for a little while before we keep going. It's been a long day. Tell you what; I'll buy you strawberry waffles if you want?"

She sat up, the neon lights from the roadside restaurant stabbing her eyes. "No thanks, I'll just have a few cups of coffee."

Weston kissed her cheek and she grabbed him, pressing her lips against his. When they broke apart, he wore a boyish smile.

"What was that for?" he asked.

"What? I can't kiss you whenever I want?"

"No not at all, it's just you don't usually kiss me like that."

She slapped his thigh playfully. "Come on; let's get you some waffles before you starve."

He rubbed his belly again. "Amen to that."

After Weston locked the car, they approached the Waffle House. Catherine noticed only two cars were in the parking lot, a red truck and a Honda Civic.

"This joint is hopping tonight," she giggled.

He took her hand and opened the door for her.

Inside, the restaurant was deserted. Nobody was at the register or behind the grill. The smell of recently cooked bacon hung in the air and made their mouths water.

"Are they even open?" she whispered. She'd always had a fear of empty spaces, especially if they were commercial. Restaurants were expected to be busy with life, not vacant and quiet. She saw a television on the wall broadcasting the local news, but the mute button was on.

"Hello, is anyone here?" Weston called out.

Dragging feet echoed from the back, followed by a guttural moan.

Catherine almost expected a walking corpse to greet them; it wasn't far from the truth. The cook, dead-tired, and looking like a zombie, came out. He was tall, fat, and had greasy curly hair poking out from behind an orange Tennessee baseball hat.

"Hi folks. Missy, your waitress, will come round front in a second. I'll take your order if you're ready."

"Coffee, please," Catherine stated, taking a seat at a booth near the door.

"We'll have two orders of strawberry waffles and a side of bacon, please," Weston said, sitting across from her.

"Can do, I'll get cooking, Missy'll bring your coffee in a moment," the cook said, and turned back toward the grill.

Catherine hid a smile. Weston caught it, guessing her thoughts about the odd man. He took her hand from across the syrup-encrusted table.

"How much farther exactly do we have to go until we get to the cabin?"

"Not far, don't worry," she said.

"How come you've never mentioned the cabin before?"

She rolled her eyes. "I didn't see much of a need. It was my parent's cabin; I just never had the heart to sell it. I've had a few offers on the property but something always holds me back. You'll enjoy it up there, it's quiet and we can go fishing on the lake." Catherine stopped talking and seemed to drift off.

"What is it?"

"Nothing," she said, but could tell what he really wanted to ask her. He wanted to know how long they would be staying at the cabin. How long until their lives could return to normal. She honestly didn't know, and promised herself not to think about it until dawn. Tonight was just for the two of them. She planned to offer herself to him tonight, and she knew by the way he stared into her eyes that he would accept.

A pot of steaming coffee jarred her thoughts as it floated near her head. She looked up to see the waitress holding it. The waitress, a petite brown-haired girl in a short skirt, poured them each a cup of coffee, then left with a smile.

"Thank you, Missy," Catherine said, raising her voice so the waitress could hear her.

Missy continued toward the back of the restaurant, as she quickly disappeared around the corner.

"That was weird, she didn't say anything," Catherine said, shaking her head. She took one of the ceramic mugs and handed one to Weston. "Not very talkative I guess."

Weston eyed the cook, but he was busy flipping waffles.

"Maybe we interrupted a phone call from her boyfriend," Weston joked.

"Yeah, maybe."

Weston snickered as he poured sugar into his coffee.

Catherine added sugar from a packet as well as some creamer. The brew was hot and strong, and she knew if she drank at least two cups she'd be able to stay up all night. Not that she needed much help in that department. The day had been filled with enough jumps and scares to keep her mind wide awake for days. She only hoped they'd be safe in the cabin.

The cook put a steaming plate of strawberry waffles and four slices of bacon on the counter and called out, "Order up!" He waited for a moment for Missy to return. When she didn't, he shuffled to the back and yelled at the girl to serve the paying customers.

Catherine drank more coffee and tried to avoid staring at the cook. He was a glutton but had a kind face and strong, working hands, she wouldn't be surprised if he had a day job digging trenches or knocking down dilapidated buildings with a bulldozer. She always admired a hard working man and tried to give them a friendly smile when she saw one. Weston was very hard working, but wasn't the type of guy she normally found herself dating. He was nice, dependable, didn't work with his hands, and was in all stereotypes a white collar worker. Nothing was wrong with that of course, she was falling more and more in love with him everyday. And he knew he could protect her by the way he'd yanked her out of the Buick.

"What's on your mind?" Weston grinned, sheepishly as he took a sip of his coffee.

"I was just thinking about how you saved me today, you were very heroic."

Weston's face reddened. "Don't mention it, maybe you can save me the next time it happens."

Catherine laughed and squeezed his hand. Everything was going to be fine as long as they had each other to see them through. She leaned in to kiss him, but was suddenly cut off.

The plate of waffles slammed down between them, sending a shockwave through the table.

Catherine had had enough of the rudeness. She curled her lip and started to rise from her seat. "Now look, Missy, you've got a lot of nerve..."

The waitress glared down at her, staring, with large black eyes.

"What seems to be the problem?" Missy asked, though her razor-thin mouth never moved.

Catherine sank into her seat, shaking.

Weston froze, not believing what he was seeing.

Without another word, the waitress turned around and walked away.

"What's going on here?" Weston gasped. He jumped up and followed after Missy. "Hey, you bug-eyed freak, get back here! I've got a few questions for you!"

The waitress spun around and the large black eyes were gone, replaced with the green ones of a perfectly natural face.

"I'm sorry, mister. I've had a really bad night. Dinner's on me, okay," she mumbled, and stormed out of sight.

Weston watched her go, his feet encased in concrete. "What the hell?"

Then Catherine was beside him, her hand on his arm.

"Let's get out of here, please."

"Yeah, that's a good idea," he agreed.

They were headed for the exit when the cook stopped them. He held a frying pan in one hand, a spatula in the other, and a fierce expression on his face.

"What's wrong with you people? Missy's paying for your meal and you're not even gonna eat it?"

Weston urged Catherine in front of him, far away from the cook and the waitress who was now watching them.

"We're not hungry anymore, sorry." He rushed out of the Waffle House with Catherine before him and they were driving out of the parking lot before the front door of the restaurant was fully closed. Weston saw the cook step out of the Waffle House in his rearview mirror, his expression one of confusion as he watched the car speed away.

Catherine whimpered and closed her eyes, shaking her head in disbelief.

"We're okay, we're fine," Weston explained to her and himself.

"We're not fine," Catherine muttered. "What the hell just happened back there? She was...she looked..."

Weston got in the fast lane and sped down the highway. He could see the Smoky Mountains ahead, rising out of the ground like the knuckles of a gigantic monster trying to escape the earth.

Catherine couldn't stop shaking. She turned the heat up in the car. "You saw her as well as I did. She had big, solid black eyes. She was one of them," she said.

"No. I don't think she was. I think we were supposed to believe she was, but it was a lie, like a Halloween costume, only she could hide it under her skin."

Catherine let out a manic laugh. "We're losing our minds."

Weston didn't look at her. He focused on driving. Once they reached the cabin they'd be safe.

"How much further is it?" he asked.

"Take the exit after this one, and then we'll take a few back roads," she said as she stared out her window and into the night sky. She searched the heavens for a blue light but found nothing, only the twinkling stars and the terrible knowledge that something out there wanted her dead.

CHAPTER EIGHT

Weston eyed the lonely dirt road suspiciously. It wasn't that he didn't trust Catherine, but the absolute isolation from humanity that the darkness offered was unsettling. The minute he drove down the road, the trees would surround them, cutting down their visibility and hiding anyone or anything that might be waiting to sneak up on them.

"What are you waiting for?" Catherine asked. "Drive."

"Are you sure this is a good idea? I mean, what if they follow us? We'll be trapped here with nowhere to run and nobody to turn to for help."

"It's safer than your apartment and definitely more secure than my house," she explained. "And we'll also have a stockpile of guns."

Weston sighed, knowing she was right. The four humanoids knew where they lived in the city, but had no clue about the cabin in the mountains, and even if they did know, perhaps with access to guns, the beings would regret paying the cabin a visit.

"Okay, fine, but the second something bad happens we get out of here."

"Agreed," she said.

Weston slowly drove onto the dirt road, the tires crunching under the gravel, each time sounding like fireworks were going off in the solitude. Just as he predicted, the swaying trees blotted out all perception of the night sky and the thick darkness swallowed them whole. The only thing he could focus on were the twin beams of light from the headlights shining in front of the car like beacons of false hope.

"How far in is the cabin?"

"Relax, it's just around the bend. You'll love it," she smiled and patted his thigh.

Weston was too jittery to feel relaxed. He drove around the bend, checking the side mirrors constantly for a silent stalker.

"Will you calm down a little? You're making me nervous," Catherine said. She leaned forward in her seat like an eager child. "I haven't seen this place in years."

As Weston passed the bend in the driveway, the headlights illuminated a small log cabin in a clearing. The image flashed for a moment then the darkness took it away.

"There it is," Catherine smiled as memories of her childhood flooded her mind.

The car crumpled the tall weeds as he attempted to find a suitable parking spot as close to the cabin as possible. He settled for a dead area of grass near a withered oak which had a tire swing hanging from one branch.

Catherine leaped from the car. She ran her fingertips over the overgrowth until she reached the tire swing. Grabbing the rope, she hoisted herself onto the tire.

"I don't think that's such a good idea," Weston complained as he exited the car. "It looks pretty old."

"Don't be silly. Come over here and give me a push."

He shook his head as he watched her. *What is she thinking? We have a group of killers who want to core out my head and she wants to play around on a damn swing!*

"Hurry up," she called as she rocked back and forth, but couldn't get enough momentum to swing herself.

"What if the branch breaks?" he said as she walked over to her. "We're far from a hospital."

She laughed at him.

"What? What's so funny?"

"You sound like my mom," she said as she leaned back, her hair falling from her face.

"What...no I don't."

"Yes, you do," she laughed. "Why don't you give me one push, just one?"

Weston crossed his arms.

"Please, Weston."

"All right," he gave in. "Just one push."

He placed his hands on her shoulder and gave her a push.

She laughed and smiled, looking like a little girl. Soon, Weston was laughing, too, the happiness infectious.

"Push me harder," she demanded.

He grabbed her waist and shoved. She flew forward, cheering all the way then came back at him. He tried to stop her, but she slammed into him, knocking him to the ground.

"Oh my God, I'm so sorry," she said and jumped off the tire swing. She took his hand and helped him to his feet. "You should've moved out of the way. Don't you know, what goes up must come down."

"Yeah, I figured that."

She kissed his cheek and walked him toward the cabin.

"Come on," she urged. "I'll give you the grand tour."

He climbed the porch steps with her and had an unsettling feeling as he took the small structure in.

"The cabin is over thirty years old, but it's comfortable, trust me," she said.

"The last time I trusted you, I landed on my back."

She played with the end of his shirt. "Well, maybe next time you won't mind being on your back."

Weston's eyes widened and she gave him a knowing smile. They had never been together that way, in fact, they have never gone past second base, and now they were going to finally consummate their relationship. He felt heat rush to his face and was glad it was so dark outside so she couldn't see him blush.

"What's wrong? Don't you want me?" she purred as she nestled herself closer to him. She nibbled his neck as her hand slid down to his crotch.

Weston moaned softly.

They stayed on the porch for a while, kissing and fondling in the dark, and then entered the cabin. She led him directly to the bedroom and closed the door.

It took only a few minutes to change the sheets to some fresh ones found in a bureau drawer, and then she showed him how loving she could be.

The young couple was occupied well into the night.

*   *   *

Lying on his back in the bed, Weston was both tired and satisfied. He watched the trees outside the window sway with the wind and couldn't believe his fortune. Catherine was curled up beside him, sleeping soundly. She'd been wild, totally absorbed in their passion. He had never expected her to be so uninhibited and sexy once she finally let her guard down. She had always been so shy and never very forceful on their dates together. She was hesitant to kiss him on the lips and her voice was always soft. But tonight had shattered every conception of her he'd ever known. She was eager, willing, and loud, and he'd enjoyed every second of it. He saw a thin streak of moonlight peer in through the window and wondered if anyone had heard them. She told him they were far removed from society so deep in the mountains; the nearest neighbor being some five miles away. He took a deep breath, happy to be alive as he caressed her face.

The thin sliver of moonlight vanished, as though someone had walked by.

Weston rose from the bed, and feeling naked and vulnerable, he slipped on his pants and went to the window. He listened for signs of an intruder such as crushed leaves, shuffling footsteps, or a restless shadow. But he heard and witnessed none of those things, only the swaying trees sighing as the darkness stared back at him. He was just about to wrap it up to nerves and go back to sleep when his cell phone rang.

Catherine stirred in her sleep.

He went to the nightstand and picked it up, pressing the call button as he pressed it to his ear.

A strange, high-pitched whistle came from the other end then a familiar voice of a man he couldn't quite place began speaking.

"What does the spider say to the fly before it sucks the insect dry?" the voice asked.

"I...I don't know? Who is this?" Weston asked.

"Does he tell it that everything will be fine, that it will only hurt a little bit? Maybe he tells the fly nothing and tries to finish it off as quickly as possible."

Weston gulped. The voice on the other end was waiting for an answer.

"What the hell do you want from us?" he whispered.

"They're searching for you. They don't know where you are right now, but I do," the voice said. "The woman has something they want, something the fly can slay the spider with."

Realization washed over him as he recalled when and where he'd heard the voice before. It was outside the Knoxville Police Department. The figure with the solid blue eyes who had flashed images into his mind, but also spoke in a cryptic way his conscious memory didn't pick up on, but his subconscious had.

"What do we have? Tell me," Weston demanded.

That odd high frequency returned and Weston pulled the phone from his ear until it stopped. When it was through, he placed it to his ear once more

"Both of you need to meet me at Hangover Bridge at four o' clock. If you don't know where it is, the woman will."

Weston started to ask a question but the line went dead. He put the phone down and looked toward the woman he'd fallen in love with. Catherine was on her stomach, her smooth back exposed above the thick blanket. He crawled back into bed and ran his palm down her spine, causing her to moan softly

"Catherine, wake up?" he said as he continued to caress her backside.

"Mmmm?"

"Come on, I need you to wake up."

She tensed, feeling the worry in his voice. She curled up on her knees and faced him, her breasts two perfect mounds.

"My cell rang and it was someone who knows what's going on."

"But how did they find us?"

"They didn't, at least not yet. They already had my cell number no doubt."

Catherine hugged him.

"The voice said you have something they want. Do you know what that might be?"

Catherine shivered in his arms. "No, who was it?" she asked.

"I think it was the figure I talked to outside the Police Station."

"Weston, what are we gonna do?"

He held her closer, comforting her, letting her feel safe. "The voice wants us to go to Hangover Bridge at four and asked for you to bring something that can stop them. What is it?"

Catherine nuzzled her head into his chest. "I don't know, lets go back to sleep."

He shook her. "Catherine, this isn't a game, tell me what you have that they want so bad?"

She began laughing but then stopped as she thought of something.

"Wait, there is one thing but...no, it's crazy."

"What is it, just tell me."

She was still talking, but not to him, she was talking to herself now. "That's why this is happening? That's what they want from me...from you?" Her body shook as a hysterical laugh turned into a sob. "I barely even watched the whole recording. I thought it was a hoax."

"What is it? Please, tell me, Catherine."

She sobered up as she remembered something and began to tremble in his embrace. She didn't answer for a few moments. Weston soothed her with his hands and kissed her on the forehead as he coaxed her to tell him what she knew.

Finally, she told him what she was thinking.

"Last year, a body came into the funeral home with a suitcase. He was an older man who'd been mutilated by either a soldering gun or a medical laser. His tongue, eyes, stomach, and genitals were missing, and his rectum was hollowed out through his small intestine. I didn't think much of it at the time. We always had bodies of murdered victims coming in to be embalmed; it was my job as you already know. I patched the body up as well as I could and put the suitcase into storage. Months flew by and nobody ever claimed it. The funeral director told me to throw it out, but I never got around to it." She shivered at the thought.

Weston pulled the blanket around her shoulders and said, "Go on, it's okay."

"Okay. So I found the suitcase a few weeks ago and decided to bring it home. I thought I'd see if there was anything in it I could donate to Goodwill. When I got home and opened it, I found some dress shirts, pants and socks, and a DVD inside it. I put the clothing aside, planning on dropping it off at one of those charity boxes. Feeling curious, I watched the DVD. I figured it would be an adult movie or maybe a training video for his work, you know, something that would tell me who the man had been, but it was some kind of home movie of a busy city street. The camera must've been a handheld because the picture had a really jerky motion to it. Deciding it wasn't anything that mattered, I was just about to turn it off when the person holding the camera zoomed in on two people walking down the street. It was a man and woman, both wearing long coats and hats; they kept their heads down and the camera couldn't see their faces. The camera operator—I assumed it was the man I'd embalmed—followed the couple into a book store. The two figures went to a shelf, pulled out a book about UFOS and laughed together, but it wasn't really laughter, it was like the way laughter sounds on a recorder." Catherine paused to catch her breath. "Can you get me something cold to drink, please? My throat is sore."

Weston kissed her and slid off the bed. She wrapped herself in the blanket, fighting off the chill. He returned a minute later with a glass of ice water.

"Thank you," she said, and drank the water down quickly.

"Were they like the others?" he asked.

"Yes," she said. "I think so."

"What happened then?" Weston pressed.

"They just kept going through more books and pointing things out that were wrong with them, you know, UFOs. The camera man continued filming for at least another five minutes. Then they stopped and turned to look right at the camera. The camera immediately was lowered and pointed at the floor, and a second later the camera man was running out of the store and across the street, cursing that he'd been spotted. He hid in a coffee shop and continued filming until the couple left the book store. But that's when things got really weird. The couple spotted him and started walking toward him. He ran to his car and drove away. The tape went to static after that and when the picture returned he was outside of an apartment complex and it was night. He was trying to film through a window but the blinds were drawn and he couldn't see anything. I remember he kept whispering about someone inside, a friend maybe. Then there was movement behind the blinds and screaming came from inside, but it stopped quickly. The camera was shaking like the man was scared out of his mind and then this long grey hand parted the blinds and an oval head with the biggest, blackest eyes I've ever seen stared right into the camera lens. The man filming started yelling and running and then it went to static," she said, her voice shaking a little. "I thought it was all some kind of joke, like a college campus prank."

Weston held her close as he considered the story he'd just been told. "Where's the DVD now?" he asked.

"It's in my purse. It's been in there since the night I watched it. I haven't known what to do with it. I was either going to throw it out and pretend I never saw it or take it to the police."

"We can't give it to the police," he said. "That has to be what the voice on the phone said you have, what else could it be? Lucky you still have it with you, too. We'll bring the DVD tonight, give it to whoever is there to meet us, and be done with this whole mess."

Catherine slid from his embrace. "How can you be so sure they'll be so forgiving? We don't even know who was on the phone or what we're dealing with here."

Weston caressed her bare shoulders but she shook him off.

"But, don't you just want to go back home?" he asked. "We can pretend none of this ever happened and get on with our lives...together."

She shook her head. "It's not that easy. I can't just pretend this never happened. We've stumbled on something huge here, and you want to hide under your bed instead of facing it head on? What are those *things*? What are they doing here? What do they want? Is this all actually real or is it just some elaborate hoax. Aren't you the least bit curious?"

Weston considered her barrage of questions but in his heart he was perfectly content with never seeing one of those beings ever again. They had torn his world apart in mere seconds, the very existence of them prompting a response. But what that response was he didn't know.

Catherine sensed him struggling and put her head on his shoulder. "Look, we don't have the luxury of not believing, we've seen too much already. If this is all real then we can't just ignore it."

"I still think we should meet whoever called me. They might be able to give us the answers we need," he said.

Suddenly, she leaped from the bed as if he'd slapped her.

"What is it?" he asked, his easy darting back and forth, searching for signs of danger.

"Wait a second, Weston. How *exactly* did you talk to the voice on the phone?" she questioned.

"I told you, my cell rang and I picked it up."

Catherine began to look very scared and Weston felt it, too, though he didn't know why.

"What's wrong? Tell me, please," he prompted, this time more forcefully.

"Weston...the cabin doesn't have any cell service, not way out here in the mountains, there aren't any cell towers."

"No, that can't be."

Weston picked up his cell phone and checked for service and was shocked to see he had no bars. There wasn't as much as a hint of a signal. There was absolutely no way he could make or receive a call way out in the middle of nowhere.

As to how he had received that phone call, he had absolutely no explanation.

CHAPTER NINE

Weston stood outside of the car holding a pump action shot-gun. Catherine's father had stored the firearm at the cabin because her mother wouldn't allow it in their other home. He tightened his grip on the walnut stock and searched Hangover Bridge for the visitor. The shotgun felt heavy in his hands. He'd never fired a gun before and couldn't imagine the outcome if he had to use it.

He checked his watch for the third time in as many minutes. It was almost four o' clock.

Hangover Bridge groaned as a strong gust of winter wind hit it. The timbers were old but strong and all he had was faith that it wouldn't fall apart while he stood on it.

Weston saw a brief shadow slip away near the end of the bridge; it happened so fast he thought his mind was playing tricks on him. He looked over at Catherine as she waited in her car. She had insisted on keeping the motor running, and waited in the driver's seat. She wasn't taking any chances and Weston couldn't blame her. He just wanted to hand over the DVD and end this once and for all.

A tall shape appeared from out of the darkness in a flutter of movement. As the figure moved closer, Weston could see it was the same one he'd met before. The figure didn't bother to hide its oval blue eyes, yet still wore a long trench coat and wide-brimmed hat.

Weston aimed the shotgun at the strange being as it approached. The humanoid figure halted a few feet away and when it spoke, it sounded like a recording of human speech, a stolen sound which elicited chills along Weston's spine.

"Do you wish to kill me?" it asked, the words real this time and not in Weston's head. Weston locked eyes with the being in front of him. For the first time, he sensed its loneliness and discontent in this world. It was hard to deny what he saw with his own eyes.

"No," Weston said, lowering the shotgun. "We're just afraid. We don't understand what's been happening to us."

The tall humanoid moved closer to him and Weston backed up until his backside touched the car.

"Do not fear me. I am here to help you," the figure said.

"Do you have a name?" Weston asked.

The figure seemed momentarily confused. "I have no name. We are one, a single race and mind."

"Okay, fine. Then where are the others?"

"They are here...on this Earth. We are united...yet apart."

"Why are you here? Who...what are you?"

The figure leaned into him, seeking to end the conversation by dazzling Weston with its hypnotic eyes. Flashes of other worlds, other galaxies, formed in Weston's mind. A planet of water, dark, and covered in ice appeared in his thoughts. Under the ice and deep in the waters was a massive city as were others.

"I don't understand. Is that your planet?" Weston asked.

"No," answered the being. "It is yours."

Weston clenched his fists. "I don't understand."

"You're confused?" it asked.

"Yes."

"Then you must understand, our minds work differently, and even if I showed you the truth of your planet and the parallel dimensions between them, it would only confuse and frustrate you more."

Weston looked away from the figure, knowing it was right. How could he possibly understand an alien intelligence? Even if he could fathom a part of its structure, he could never see the entire picture, only the fragmented pieces of the puzzle.

He put the shotgun on the trunk of the car and dug into his coat pocket.

"I have what you're looking for."

The humanoid was suddenly closer, looming over Weston greedily. Weston fingered the DVD in its jewel case before taking it out.

"Once I give this to you, I have your word that you'll leave us alone?" he asked.

The being's head bobbed up and down in a jarring, bird-like motion.

"And what about the others, the black eyed ones that have been following me and my girlfriend?"

The being stopped nodding. "I cannot promise they won't harm you, the harvest is drawing near."

"What harvest?"

"The Greys are entitled to this world."

Weston shuttered at the sudden memory of the four humanoids trying to kidnap Catherine, the Buick speeding away when they failed.

"What do they want?" he asked.

The figure lifted its four-fingered hand and put it on Weston's shoulder. He flinched when the tapered fingers clamped down like a vise and wouldn't release.

"It is better you do not know," the figure replied in its hollow voice. "Hand over what you brought me, now."

Weston stared into the deep, blue eyes and couldn't break free of them. He handed over the DVD without further delay. The figure released its hold and pulled away.

"Thank you. We will keep in touch."

"What about our deal?" Weston asked.

The tall figure began to move away as it faded into the darkness, only its eyes appearing in the night. The sight reminded Weston of the Cheshire cat from *Alice in Wonderland.*

"Wait, I have more questions. How long have you been here? Why are you doing this?" he called but the eyes vanished, his questions unanswered.

Weston stared at the bridge, searching for the figure, but there was nothing to see except darkness and the metal railings lining the bridge. The being, whatever it might be, was gone.

The car horn beeped. Catherine revved the engine, eager to leave. Weston picked up the shotgun from off the hood and climbed into the passenger's seat. He closed the door and wouldn't face Catherine's questioning glare.

"Well, did he take it?"

"He might not be the right word to describe what that thing was but, yes, *he* did. Now let's get out of here."

Catherine put the car in drive and slowly rolled off the bridge. Hangover Bridge was swallowed by the night as Catherine drove onto the road and began to accelerate. She gripped the steering wheel with both hands and rolled down the window for some fresh air.

Weston took comfort in the cold blasts of air pouring through the car; it cooled him down and remained a strong reminder that they were making distance between them and the tall being somewhere in the woods behind them.

"What did he...it, say to you?"

"Nothing. I mean, it didn't actually speak, I couldn't hear it."

"What do you mean? Couldn't hear it speaking?"

"No, I tried, but its lips never moved, never made a sound." Weston rubbed his eyes in frustration.

"But it spoke, I heard it. It sounded like a voice on the radio, only different."

"How was it different?"

"I don't know, damn it." Catherine left him alone then and focused on the road ahead.

"I'm sorry," Weston apologized. He put his hand on her thigh, testing the waters to make sure she understood he didn't mean to snap at her. She didn't move his hand so he figured he was in the clear.

"It told me some very disturbing things," he said.

"Like what?"

He replayed the entire scenario for her and didn't leave out a single detail. By the time they arrived back at the cabin, he was breathing heavily and Catherine had turned pale.

"He didn't explain what they were harvesting?" she asked after hearing the story.

"No, and I really don't think we want to know. Maybe it doesn't concern us."

Her face grew hard as she said, "Doesn't concern us? Weston, those beings—whether they're from outer space or another dimension or are just psychopaths—are killing people. How can you say it's no concern of ours when we can put a stop to it?"

"Catherine, it's over. We gave it what it wanted and now we can get back to our lives. It's all over."

She frowned at him and crossed her arms over her chest. "And what about those teenagers that were murdered near my house? Can you honestly tell their parents and friends that they didn't die in vain, that nobody else will suffer because we knew what was going on and did nothing to stop it?"

Weston lowered his voice, not waiting to turn this into a full-fledged argument.

"But you don't know if they're responsible for that act," he said.

She shoved his hand off her thigh and climbed out of the car, slamming the door.

"Catherine, wait a second," he called.

She ignored him, stormed up the cabin's porch steps, faced the front door to the cabin, and froze as she stared off into the woods.

Weston followed her, slowly, considering his words before speaking them.

Maybe she's right. Maybe we should go to the cops and tell them what we know. Yeah, right, and they'd believe us? We'd be locked up and then thrown in an asylum.

"Weston, I think someone's watching us," she said, pointing toward the woods.

"Stay here, I'll go look." He went and retrieved the shotgun, and when he walked around the porch and reached the edge of her house, he was startled by what he found.

A man wearing full camouflage and holding a rifle was looking directly at him.

"Hello, who is that?" Weston called out.

The trees parted and a tall, muscular man stepped out. In the dim glow of the security lights, he seemed grim and deadly, but the rifle was aimed at the ground which immediately calmed Weston.

"Hi there. The name's Greg Carlson. I didn't mean to alarm you. I was hunting for deer and saw a weird blue light in the woods. I thought a plane had crashed or something so I came to investigate it."

"Well, you were wrong. Nothing crashed around here. Now please leave my property," Catherine said. She unlocked the front door, stepped inside, and closed it.

Weston matched stares with the man.

"Awfully sorry, pal, I meant you or your lady no harm," the hunter said.

"It's been a long night, sorry about that, normally she's very polite."

Greg looked over at the cabin. "So, you really didn't see that blue light?"

"You should leave now," Weston replied, ignoring the man's question.

"Fine, well, good night then," Greg said, turned, and faded back into the woods.

Weston took a seat on the porch after the man was gone. He watched the morning sun creep across the sky and wondered if his and Catherine's ordeal was finally over.

CHAPTER TEN

After having a quick dinner, both Catherine and Weston went to bed.

At first they merely held each other, talking about what had happened and what their future might hold. In time, they began to caress one another and before either knew it, they were lost in each others arms, nothing but the heavy breathing and moans of pleasure filling their ears.

Afterward, Weston kissed her one last time and rolled over to fall asleep. Catherine lay beside him, listening to him breathe, and then she too fell asleep.

No sooner did she fall into a deep slumber than she began to dream.

In her dream, she was standing beside a dark-haired girl on a busy sidewalk in a city she'd never been in before. Tall buildings grew like redwoods on all sides, and people were everywhere; walking in and out of stores, and continually moving as many talked on cell phones and carried briefcases and leather bags. The girl was waiting for someone, but Catherine wasn't sure who or why.

She spotted an old Buick making its way toward her as it weaved in and around the traffic. She wanted to run but couldn't, something was holding her back. She had the distinct impression that this wasn't really happening to her, that this was the past of another victim, much like the dream she'd had of the woman who had drowned in the lake.

The Buick pulled up to the sidewalk and stopped. Two figures in dark sunglasses and trench coats slipped out from the back seat. One lowered its glasses enough for her to see the soulless, black eyes residing underneath.

"Run! Get out of here!" Catherine screamed at the girl standing beside her, but to Catherine's horror, the girl took a step closer to the Buick.

One of the figures spoke to her using telepathy.

"Where is the audio recording?"

"Hidden," the girl smirked. "You won't get away with this. I'll expose all of you," she said, her defiance obvious to anyone listening.

The two figures continued to stare at her.

"What are you going to do?" the girl asked "Abduct me on a busy New York street at rush hour?" She seemed so confident in her assessment of the situation, that nothing bad could happen here, that she was in a safe place.

Catherine knew otherwise. She knew the figures with the black eyes had no fear. They were beyond the reach of the laws of man and harbored the inner secrets of space and time. The girl was no match for them. It was only a matter of time before they made a move to take her.

"Get out of here," the girl jeered. "And don't come back again."

The two figures moved quickly, becoming all but a blur. Catherine blinked her eyes and in that time they had the girl by the wrists and were shoving her into the Buick. The girl screamed for all she was worth, but the roaring traffic and ambient noise drowned out her cries. Then a four-fingered hand cupped her mouth, silencing her and a sharp instrument tore through her shirt and bra. Another device shaped like a sickle sliced off her jeans and panties. The figures worked fast, shoving the instrument beneath her rib cage. The girl's eyes bulged as they separated flesh, muscle, and bone within the span of seconds. One of them ran a square panel over her intestines and suddenly her organs were exposed. They emptied her, tossing the liver, kidneys, heart, lungs, and ropey intestines onto the floor. She was hollowed out quickly and thrown out of the Buick like trash. As the body slapped the ground, the Buick sped down the street and out of view.

Catherine stared down at the lifeless corpse at her feet. People began to crowd around the bloody corpse, questioning each other about what had happened and why.

"You're just a bunch of fucking sheep! How could you miss what just happened to her?" Catherine screamed at them.

The crowd ignored her as they chatted amongst themselves about the grisly scene.

Catherine let loose a loud shriek at the unfairness of the world, as she screamed for the dead girl, and for herself.

* * *

"Catherine, wake up, God, you're having a nightmare," Weston was saying as he shook her awake.

Catherine awoke in the bedroom of the cabin with tears streaming down her cheeks.

A...dream... it was just a dream, she thought as she blinked a few times and tried to push the awful images away.

"Wow, you were having another nightmare and this one seemed worse than the last one."

"Tell me about it," she groaned and rolled out of bed. "What I don't know is why I'm having them."

"Do you remember what it was about?" he asked.

She thought back to the dream, pieces of it already slipping away, but the girl being systematically mutilated was still there, crystal clear, and she closed her eyes as she shook her head. She felt Weston's hand on her back as he waited for her to reply.

"It was only a bad dream. Dreams can't hurt you," he told her.

She rose from the bed and began to pace back and forth. She wanted to tell him about the girl the Greys killed, how real it seemed, but she didn't say anything. No, not yet! Not until she knew it was true and not just a figment of her subconscious. Besides, he had already been through so much that she...

"Catherine, are you okay? You seem a little dazed."

She was pulled from her thoughts and said, "I'm fine, just a little shaken up. It was some dream, I remember that much," she replied. She didn't think she was going to be going back to sleep anytime soon and her nightclothes were covered in sweat so she headed for the bathroom. "I'll be in the shower, pack our things, please. I want to leave."

"What? Why?"

"Because, Weston, we're going back home. We can't stay here."

He shook his head. "I don't understand."

"You don't have to, just trust me, it's time to go."

She closed the bathroom door and took a towel from the back if it, draping it over the closed toilet. She heard him muttering about how insane it was that they leave but she ignored it. He knew he wouldn't want to leave the cabin and return to his apartment and she could understand that. She didn't want to go back to an empty home either. But something in her dream, something she couldn't put her finger on, told her they needed to leave.

Maybe they could live together for a few weeks until everything was finally over. She wouldn't mind coming home to see Weston's smiling face each night either.

She slipped out of her nightclothes, turned on the hot water, and stepped under the shower's nozzle. It was cold at first but in a few seconds the electric water heater kicked in and the water grew warm. It never got really hot but it was better than the outside temperature.

The steaming spray of water felt like a million little fingers massaging her. She let the water course through her hair, down her spine, and her slender legs.

She sighed as tense muscles relaxed; a hot shower was just what she needed.

Steam fogged the sliding glass door of the shower stall, and the bathroom was soon covered in wisps of billowing fog. She picked up the soap and immediately dropped it when she saw an oval face peer at her from behind the fogged sliding glass.

"Get away from me. Get out of here!" she screamed as her heart jack hammered in her chest and she began to panic. They were here! Oh, God, they were here and had come to kill her!

Large, black eyes stared through the steam at her, beckoning her to escape.

She placed her palm against the glass, pushing with all her might in case the intruder tried to get in.

"Catherine?" Weston asked as he gently tapped on the bathroom door. "Is everything all right?"

The figure suddenly vanished as if it had never been there. She blinked her eyes, wondering if she had truly seen it or if her mind was torturing her.

Had the Grey been there at all or was she losing what sanity she had left?

The bathroom door opened and Weston rushed in. He looked around, found the bathroom empty, and scratched his head as to what the yelling was about.

"I'm fine..." she said, holding back sobs of fear. "I just thought I saw something, but I'm okay now. It was all a mistake."

"Okay, if you're sure. Remember, I'm just outside the door if you need me. Yell and I'll be in a second later." He turned to leave.

"No, wait," Catherine said as she stood before him, naked, the hot water sluicing down her body. "Stay with me, till I'm done."

He closed the bathroom door and sat on the toilet as he let his eyes gaze over her supple form. He felt his arousal growing as he admired her curves but ignored it, knowing this wasn't the time. He knew she'd had a scare of some kind and he wanted to be there for her, not act like a horny boyfriend looking for an excuse for sex. "I packed everything. We can leave when you're ready," he said as he looked away from her, staring at his feet.

"We don't have to go right this second," she said. "And I could use some one to wash my back."

He saw the sensual smile she now wore and he grinned boyishly. It took him less than three seconds to strip off his clothes and join her in the shower.

Five minutes later, Catherine's eyes were closed once more, but this time she only had visions of passion.

CHAPTER ELEVEN

The Shady Oaks Apartments parking lot was relatively empty as Weston drove off the street. Vacant parking spots were in abundance and he took advantage of the closest one to the entrance.

"Well, we're here," he said as he turned off the engine with the flick of his wrist. He took out the ignition key and slid it into his pocket. "Though I still can't believe we left the cabin."

Catherine leaned back in her seat and sighed. "It's not so bad. We need to get on with our lives, not live in fear. Besides, they got what they wanted; they have no reason to bother us anymore."

"And what do we do about them if they don't leave us alone?"

Catherine leaned over and kissed his cheek. "If that happens, I have a plan."

He raised his eyebrows and was about to ask what this great plan of hers was when she said, "So, why don't you show me inside? I'd like to know where I'll be sleeping."

Weston forced a smile. He unpacked the car and led her up three flights of stairs.

"I hope you cleaned the place," she joked.

"I might have forgotten to buy toilet paper, but don't be alarmed." He grinned. "We have tissues, too."

He put down their luggage on his welcome mat and unlocked the front door.

"Brace yourself now. You're my first guest in a long time and the maids been off for like...forever."

Catherine laughed, charmed at his witticism.

"Then we'll just have to change that now, won't we?" She squeezed his arm and followed him inside. The apartment was cold, and a draft blew through an open window.

Catherine hugged herself. "Wow, it's freezing in here."

"Sorry," he apologized. "I guess I forgot to close one of the windows."

Catherine spotted the open window and came to an abrupt halt. "Are you sure you left it open and it's not them?"

"No, it's okay," Weston soothed her as he slammed the window closed. "I must've left it open." He pointed to the planter with a very dead plant on it. "If someone broke in they would have knocked this over and there's nothing on the carpet to indicate that. And I doubt they would have vacuumed before they left if they did."

"Are you sure?" Catherine squeaked and scanned the apartment for danger.

"Pretty much so, yeah."

"Can we search the place anyway? I just want to make sure we're alone."

"We are, don't worry."

"Weston, please. Let's have a quick look around. We've had enough surprises today."

With a sigh he opened one of the bags and took out the shotgun, then he took her hand and they went into the kitchen. He opened a drawer and gave her a knife.

"Be careful with this," he warned.

Catherine clutched the handle tight. "Oh that's fair. You get a gun and I get a knife."

"You want to trade?"

She shook her head. "No, I'm fine, I'm just saying."

He checked his small pantry and found all his can goods were still in place. A baseball bat was leaning against his laundry basket and he looked at it. His shotgun was better but it was good to know the bat was still there if needed.

"Let's go check," he whispered.

Catherine nodded. She stayed right behind him and held the knife downward so she wouldn't stab him by accident.

Weston ushered them into the living room again. He checked behind the couch, and moved toward the hallway leading to the bathroom and other rooms. He flung open the hall closet and poked around in the hanging jackets and shirts, and content, he continued onward. The bathroom was clear, and just as Weston feared, he was out of toilet paper.

"Shit, I'm sorry 'bout that."

She smiled wanly. "We'll go to the store later; it's not that big of a deal. Let's check out the other rooms so I can finally relax."

"Okay," he agreed, and led her to his home office. The room was covered on all sides by large book shelves, each shelf containing a different category: fantasy, science fiction, horror, romance, and literature. A desk and a swivel chair were in the center of the room. Weston bypassed the desk and went straight for the closet. Stacks of cardboard boxes greeted him as he flung it open.

"I think this room is clear, too," he said as he hefted the shotgun.

"Then there's only one room left to go," she said.

Weston placed the shotgun over his shoulder and strolled to his bedroom, confident his apartment was empty. He searched the bedroom closet for someone hiding behind his clothes and found nothing.

"I believe we're safe," he said. "There's no one hiding in here, just like I said."

She pointed under the bed and the way she looked gave him the impression she might've discovered something disagreeable.

Weston got on all fours and peeked under the bed. For a moment his heart skipped a beat, as he saw what looked like a large-headed creature under the bed, but when he shoved his shotgun at the figure, it came apart.

"It's just a bunch of my stuff, nothing to worry about."

Catherine knelt down beside him. She put the knife on the bed and searched under it as well. Pulling, she forced an elongated box out from under Weston's bed. To her dismay, it was shaped like a small coffin.

"What's this?"

"I can explain that," he chuckled.

She popped open the lid, revealing a dusty, green dragon puppet.

"Who's this?" she giggled, relaxing a little now that she knew they were safe.

"This..." Weston said as he took the puppet out of its coffin, "...is Seraph, The Terror of Sweetwater."

"Uh-huh, you know, most guys have porn under their beds."

"Who says that I don't?"

"Oh, you're in trouble for that one. Do I have to drag everything under there out now?"

He sat the dragon on his lap. "If you wish, but Seraph won't be pleased."

"And why won't he be pleased?" she asked.

"He won't be happy because there's a famous knight under the bed who wants to slay him." He stuffed his hand into the slit in the dragon's back, granting him life. "No, don't bring out the knight," he said in a funny voice.

Catherine laughed, hard. "Okay, now can you tell me why you have puppets under your bed?"

"They belonged to my uncle. He was a great puppeteer. Seraph was a misunderstood dragon who lived in a cave in the woods. The villagers feared him without provocation and sent the best knight they had to slay him."

"How terrible," Catherine chuckled. "And what was the brave knight's name?"

"He was called Sir Eric of Glenmoore. He found the dragon and fought him but Seraph was too powerful and won the battle. He kept the knight in his cave and nursed him back to health. Sir Eric and Seraph became friends and came to an understanding about how things aren't always how they seem. The dragon wasn't evil, he was just different."

Catherine took Seraph from Weston and sighed. "I wish real life was that simple." She placed the dragon back in his oblong box. "By the way, why is he in a coffin?"

"The show was cancelled after the first season. It was my uncle's idea to make coffins for Seraph and Sir Eric. He took the news of the cancellation pretty hard. He gave them to me before he died."

She pushed the small coffin back under the bed.

"Come on, I'll make you lunch," she said. "You do have food here, right?"

"I only have liquor and condiments," he joked. "Can I offer you a gin and tonic?"

She put her fingers through his hands. "That sounds great."

Their lips touched and she fell on top of him as she leaned in closer. Weston tumbled to the floor, Catherine straddling him, and they stayed that way, kissing feverishly and loving one another.

He slid his hands up her shirt and caressed her firm breasts.

Then she pushed herself off him, stood up, and began to straighten her clothes.

"Hey, where are you going?" he asked.

"To the kitchen, I'm starving. We'll play later," she smiled as she stepped over him.

Weston went for her ankles and missed by an inch. He watched her butt as she walked away and thought how lucky he was.

Once in the kitchen, Catherine cracked opened the refrigerator and sorted through Weston's meager food supply.

"I found some Swiss cheese and honey smoked turkey, that look like they aren't expired?" she called.

Weston jumped to his feet and walked into the hallway.

"They should be fine, just don't drink the milk." He entered the kitchen and saw her unscrewing the milk cap. "Didn't you hear me? I wouldn't do that if I were you."

She sniffed the milk and gagged. "Oh God, this is spoiled, it smells horrible. I'm pouring it down the drain."

He smiled as he watched her pour the milk, running the water to help wash it down the drain. He hadn't had anyone visit his apartment in at least a year, let alone a woman. He could get used to the idea very easily.

After she poured the chunky milk into the kitchen sink, she began to search his cupboards.

"Where are the plates?" she asked.

Weston put his hands on her small waist as he came up behind her. He kissed her neck and moved lower.

"Weston..."

"I know you're hungry, but it can wait a few seconds, can't it?" He reached beyond her and withdrew two dinner plates from the cabinet above her head.

"You do have bread, right?" she asked, ignoring his attempt at foreplay.

He pulled away from her and took out a loaf of Jewish rye from behind the toaster, feeling dejected that she didn't want to play.

"Wait, I found one more thing in the refrigerator," she grinned, mischief playing in her eyes. She held a can of whip cream and a seductive smile creased her lips. "Would you like to lick some of this off me?"

Weston's mouth hung open a little. He nodded and ran his tongue over his lips.

She laughed as she put the can up to her neck and sprayed a trail of small white puffs from there to the V in her shirt.

He went to her, kissing her lips then moving to her neck. She moaned and pulled on the back of his hair as he went lower and lower. Soon, her shirt was off and his pants were around his ankles. She bent over and began to moan as he entered her, and for the moment, the sandwiches were temporarily forgotten.

* * *

That night, as Weston slept, Catherine wrote down everything that had happened to them. She didn't skip any details, including the horrible nightmares she'd been having. When she finished, she started an internet search for the girl she saw being killed in her nightmare. At first she only discovered a few ambiguous web sites dealing with alien abductions, and the like, and a conspiracy theory about government involvement. But after a few minutes, the otherworldly face with big black eyes, no nose, and a thin mouth popped up.

She was shocked to discover that people called them Greys, claiming they came from outer space and abducted humans for some kind of reproduction experiments. She saved the brief descriptions onto Weston's hard drive and continued her search. Human mutilation and the Greys was a taboo topic and she soon found that every case was either a dead end or an unconfirmed report handed down from word of mouth. Two hours slipped by, and she was rubbing her eyes and ready to call it quits for the night, when a bizarre picture of a dissected woman on a gurney caught her attention. The horrific sight was posted on a forum dealing with the Greys' intentions, and made Catherine's blood run cold. She'd seen the woman before, the holes for eyes, surgically cored stomach, missing organs, and the silent scream frozen on the sunken face. She sucked in a quick breath; it was the woman from her nightmare, the one they kidnapped from her bedroom, vivisected, and drowned in a secluded lake.

Her free hand instantly went to her mouth as she scanned through the comments left from other people; most of them thought it was a hoax or that it was a killer with a soldering gun. They didn't know the truth and had no idea how the woman had truly suffered at the hands of the Greys.

The floor creaked behind her and Catherine spun around in the computer chair to face the darkness, the glow of the computer screen the only light in the room. The living room was empty save for the couch and television.

It was then that she noticed a window was halfway open near the balcony.

"Weston, are you there?" Her whisper seemed loud in the darkness.

She left the computer and cautiously went to the window. She felt watched, like someone was scrutinizing her. Cold air swirled around her head as she peered out the open window.

The outside world was quiet, lights were out in nearly all the apartments, and the road was devoid of traffic. She slammed the window closed and locked it.

I don't remember Weston opening this window, she thought.

She decided she would question him on the matter in the morning. Besides, it was too late to worry about it now and he was fast asleep. In fact, she could hear him snoring if she listened hard enough. She saved the information on the computer and powered down the system. Before the computer took away all the available light, she scurried back to the bedroom and closed the door. She couldn't afford to be careless, not anymore, not ever again.

Her eye caught the glint of metal on the other side of the bed and she knew it was the shotgun leaning against the nightstand.

She slid into the bed, curled herself against Weston, and with his steady breathing to listen to, she was asleep within minutes.

As she slept, she was unaware of the tall shadow which loomed over her and Weston's sleeping forms.

CHAPTER TWELVE

Catherine awoke to bright morning sunshine. She stretched out in the bed and realized Weston was missing. Spotting a note near the alarm clock, she sat up and clumsily read it.

Catherine,

I went to work. I'll be home at five. There's eggs in the fridge. I didn't want to wake you, as you looked so peaceful and beautiful. Feel free to call me on my cell if you like and I'll see you when I get off work.

Love, Weston

P.S. Something is wrong with my computer so don't try to check your email.

She went rigid when she read the last of the note, and wondered if the data she'd saved had contained a virus. But that would have to wait for now, she had more pressing matters to attend to.

First, she called in sick for work, her boss sounded genuinely concerned because she almost never called in. She complained about a fever and stomach cramps, and was let off the hook.

After that, she went to the kitchen for breakfast. Weston told her he cooked but never said how often. She found the eggs on a plate where he said they would be.

Soon, the smell of cooking eggs and toast filled the apartment and she found herself liking the role of a housewife, though she was still an independent woman.

She was already thinking about what she would do to Weston when he returned home, her sexual drive in high gear now that she was actually getting some. As she tried to make up her mind what to do, she put a forkful of the eggs into her mouth. Her taste buds soared to new heights, the eggs were delicious and she swallowed every bite, surprised at how hungry she was.

She washed down her breakfast with a glass of orange juice and heard something dripping in the hallway; it reminded her of a leaky facet falling into a pool of water. She set her glass down and went to investigate.

Drip! Drip! Drip!

The sound increased in volume as she began to search.

Is that coming from the hallway closet? she wondered.

She pressed her ear to the closet door. The dripping noise drummed in her ear, and she was about to open the door when her feet grew wet and she saw she was standing in a warm puddle. Her first instinct was to pull away as the dark pool seeped from under the closet door and into the hallway.

It was then she realized it wasn't water...it was blood!

"What the hell's going on here?"

She opened the door and couldn't breathe. Her mouth dropped open and her legs wobbled as she sank to the floor. In the closet, dangling from meat hooks, dripping blood, were the mutilated remains of three bodies. They all had one feature in common: their eyes were missing, lips removed, and a gaping hole where a stomach once resided.

Catherine kicked the door closed and ran into the bathroom, screaming. Once inside, she slammed and locked the door, pressing her shoulder against it.

"This can't be happening. This can't be happening. Oh, God, please, this isn't real, it's all in my mind," she babbled like a mantra. She pushed away from the door and sat on the toilet, her eyes never leaving the door. She expected it to begin to bulge inward and break apart at any minute as the Greys came for her. Then they would dissect her, slicing her up and pulling out her organs, only to leave her hanging in a closet like so much slaughterhouse veal.

But the door remained solid and though she dared not open the door, her mind was dizzy with thoughts of the Greys waiting for her in the hallway, their long fingers waiting to grab her.

When nothing came for her, she began to relax, if only a little. They weren't coming for her, not yet. She began to wonder if it was all a nightmare but one look at her bloody feet told her it was very real.

Tears streamed down her cheeks as she used a towel to dry her eyes. It was as she turned to look in the mirror that she realized since entering the bathroom she hadn't done so, and she choked at what was written on the mirrored surface. In bold red strokes, the words dripping long rivulets of blood beneath the letters, was a warning that made the hairs on the back of her neck stand at attention and her skin crawl.

You Are Next.

CHAPTER THIRTEEN

Weston checked his rearview mirror a second time to make sure he wasn't delusional. The old Buick was a few cars behind him and trying to catch up. There was a green light ahead that had just turned yellow and he accelerated and shot through the intersection just as the light turned red. He glanced in his rearview mirror and sighed to see the Buick was stuck behind two cars at the light.

"See you later," Weston chimed as he took a right and lost his pursuers.

But just before he took the corner, the Buick darted into the opposite lane, swerved around a Toyota that beeped in anger, and ran the red light to catch up to him.

"Damn it!" he cursed

He took a quick left and went down a side street. As he drove past a gas station, he nearly collided head on with a dump truck. He cursed himself and tried to stay in his own lane as he tried to put some distance between himself and the Buick. The dump truck blared its horn as it roared by and Weston heard his tires screech as he swerved onto Main Street and merged into traffic.

"Shit," he hissed through his teeth, as he witnessed the Buick coming up behind him. He could see four Greys wearing dark sunglasses, their straight lined mouths motionless as they closed the distance separating them.

He hit the brakes at the next light and was jerked forward as the Buick tapped his rear bumper. He heard car doors opening and slamming shut as the Greys came for him. He pressed the gas pedal to the floor and twisted the steering wheel to run the red light but the Greys blocked his escape and he had to drive on the sidewalk just to avoid crashing into other cars on the road.

Horns beeped, people shouted curses at him, and the Greys got back into the Buick as he sped off. He wondered where the hell all the police were. It figured, when he really needed a cop, none could be found.

He drove down a narrow, one-way alley, running over trashcans and sending cardboard boxes flying into the air. The alley veered onto Green Street and from there he headed for Market Square, then a busy parking garage. He passed people on their way to work, and a police cruiser. He thought about stopping and asking the cop inside the cruiser for help, but knew deep down that the law couldn't do anything to assist him.

He drove into the parking garage and ascended three levels before finding a suitable parking spot. He chose a spot so he could make a quick escape if he had to. He left the engine running and waited to see if the Buick was still on his tail. Time ticked by slowly. He dug his nails into the steering wheel in anticipation but no one showed.

A car did appear and he felt his bowels tighten, but it was only a little old lady driving an old Nova. She could barely see over the steering wheel and her gray hair fluttered in the wind under her flowered hat.

Weston guessed that he'd lost the Greys, but he didn't want to take any unnecessary chances. These beings were intelligent enough to know the precise moment to strike, and when to withdraw. He hoped at the moment, they had chosen the latter.

Fifteen minutes past before he turned off the engine and sighed in relief. He was late for work, and Blake, his boss, wouldn't be pleased. He slumped in the driver's seat wondering if he should go to work now.

If the Greys wanted him, all they had to do is wait for him to show up for work.

How long is this going to go on for? We gave them the DVD. What more do they want from me and Catherine?

In the end, he decided he couldn't live in fear. Besides, he needed to work or he wouldn't be able to make money to eat. So if he quit his job and went into hiding, it was just as good as being dead.

He stayed put for another ten minutes before deciding to head for the book store. It was busier now and cars drove by him, searching for a parking spot in the garage, but none of them were the Buick.

The only thing still bothering him was the harvest the Watcher had told him about back on the bridge. He'd said they were harvesting people but never explained why. It was a mystery he didn't want to solve, and he felt better that he had the luxury of not knowing. As long as they left Catherine and himself alone, he would be content. Hell, he couldn't save the world, but he could protect himself and Catherine.

But they're not leaving us alone. Today proves that. They're still after us...me. We've seen and know too much for their liking.

"No," he said, unwilling to give in to the primitive fear. "I won't let them control my life, not anymore." His eyes looked back at him in the rearview mirror as he tried to convince himself of the very words he said, as if by saying them out loud they were more real.

He left the safety of his vehicle and headed for the stairs which led to the street, deciding he would walk the rest of the way to work. It wasn't far, just a few blocks. He passed a woman in a business suit talking on a cell phone on his way. She was babbling about different types of makeup and how she had trouble getting rid of the blemishes on her face. Weston saw nothing wrong with her complexion as he kept walking.

How silly all of us must seem to them. Parading around like a bunch of sheep, being herded from work to home, to work and home again; everyone obeying the laws of a nine-to-five job and filling our heads with the trash on television. What obvious fools we are. They must laugh about how easily they blended into our culture, hiding behind a pair of sunglasses and a trench coat, and no one paying them a bit of attention, each self absorbed in their tiny lives. We always tell ourselves we're on the top of the food chain, the rulers of this backwater chunk of rock called Earth. I wonder how long they've been studying us, how long they'll keep us around. We've made it too easy for the wolf to hunt among the sheep.

Weston's train of thought was broken when a man in a black suit bumped into him. "Excuse me," the man said and side-stepped out of Weston's way.

"No problem," Weston replied.

The man eyed Weston suspiciously and looked ready to ask him a question, but Weston cut him off before the man could speak.

"Do you know what time it is?" Weston asked.

The man looked at his watch and then back at him. "Eight minutes before ten."

"Thank you," Weston replied, and hurried down the street. He glanced over his shoulder to see the man take out a cell phone and begin speaking. Weston quickened his pace. He walked through the busy section of Market Square then crossed onto Main Street. He could see the book store on the corner, jammed between a crowded intersection of salons and boutiques on one side and a trendy coffee shop on the other.

He arrived at work a shaken but alive. His nerves were on the fringe and by the frown Blake gave him as he entered the store; he knew it was going to be a long day.

"You're late," Blake greeted.

"I know," Weston said as he rushed into the back room to punch in. He promised Blake he would sort through the books customers had turned in for trade credit today, and get them on the shelves A.S.A.P.

Blake followed him. He was a short, thin man wearing thick glasses who rarely smiled. He reminded Weston of the man on the old Twilight Zone episode, the one who broke his glasses and couldn't read the books he wanted after the world ended.

"Someone came by this morning and left you a message," Blake said gruffly.

"Was it Catherine?" Weston asked.

"No, it was a man. He was very tall and…" Blake flustered at the memory and Weston realized he'd never seen him so distraught. "Well, anyway, here you go." Blake handed him a folded piece of notebook paper and returned to the front counter.

Weston opened the note with caution, as though it might contain a venomous coiled snake. The note was written in thick black ink and read: ***Meet me at the Miles warehouse in one hour. Come alone***. There was an address listed below the message and a hand drawn picture of two oval, eyes.

He folded the paper and shoved it into his front pocket as he considered what this might mean. He knew exactly where the warehouse was, it was an abandoned building on the bad side of downtown. It was once an industrial factory for jeans and after the company went out of business, the building had fallen into disrepair, as most of the buildings in that part of town had. He lowered his head into his hands.

The figure known as the Watcher had the DVD now, what more did it want from him? He thought back to last night, and the man he'd found in the back of Catherine's cabin. What was his name? Greg. He'd told Weston that he'd seen the blue light in the woods.

What was the Greys role in this plot and what was his?

As Weston struggled to come to grips with the unknown entities in the play of life and death he'd found himself in, Blake returned carrying a large box. He placed it onto the table and dozens of paperbacks spilled out. "Here's some more for you," he said, no smile, no snicker, just an emotionless drone worthy of a sheep.

"I have to leave in an hour," Weston said.

Blake's upper lip twitched. "What are you talking about? You just got here," he said.

"I know, but this is important. I'll make it up to you, Blake. How about I work the Saturday and Sunday shift next week?"

Blake huffed but the idea of a weekend off definitely appealed to him.

Weston had never asked Blake for anything in his time at the book store and bartering for shifts was a new avenue in their relationship.

"What's so important that you need to leave?" Blake asked.

Weston touched the edge of the note in his pocket with his fingertips. "That message you gave me was important. A friend needs my help."

Blake watched him carefully as he tried to deduce if Weston was telling the truth.

"Fine, you can go in an hour but you can't have my Saturday shift, I need the hours. You can have Sunday though."

"That's acceptable," Weston agreed, smiling slightly. "Thank you."

Blake shook his head and went back up front.

Weston took the note from his pocket and read it once more.

He didn't know what was coming at the meeting, but he could only hope he might receive a few answers for all the ever growing pile of questions he was collecting.

CHAPTER FOURTEEN

Catherine stood outside of Weston's apartment building, waiting for the police. After the initial shock of seeing the message on the bathroom mirror, she calmed herself down by taking something to calm her nerves. She stayed locked inside the bathroom for over an hour and when nobody broke down the door to get her, she figured the bodies were just a warning.

If the Greys wanted to kidnap her they could've done it easily and she now regretted leaving the cabin. As she thought of their last attempt at dragging her into the Buick, she slipped out of the bathroom and locked herself in the bedroom. From there, she called the police, and then made her way outside when she was confident no one else was in the apartment with her.

That was twenty minutes ago and the authorities still hadn't arrived.

She knew the police could be slow to respond to calls, but the time she was waiting was ridiculous. There were three dead bodies hanging in the closet for God's sake!

A black Sedan made its way down the street and finally stopped when it reached her.

Two men in black suits stepped out of the Sedan, one blond, the other bald.

"We're sorry to keep you waiting, ma'am," the blond one said. His voice was cold and stale.

She backed away, preparing to run back into the apartment building.

"I thought the police always had to show their badges and wore uniforms?"

"We are in uniform," the bald one replied, his inflection resembling a robotic voice. "Can you let us inside, please?"

Her instincts told her not to let them in. Something about the way they looked set off alarm bells in her head.

"I need to see some identification," she said.

"You can't be serious," the bald man said but his partner pulled out his wallet and flashed a badge.

"Agent Adare, 501 Division, and this is Agent Mosby. We came to investigate your claim of burglary and murder."

Catherine bit her lower lip, a habit she sometimes did when she was nervous. She'd never heard of the 501 Division, and the way they talked seemed devoid of human emotion.

"Can you show us the bodies, please, ma'am?"

"Yes," she said. "Of course, follow me." She opened the door and let them come inside. "I saw them in the hallway closet, and there's writing on the bathroom mirror."

The agents followed her down the hall and to the front door of Weston's apartment. Both of the men took off their shoes and left them by the door, which to Catherine seemed an odd thing to do given the circumstances.

"I'll stay out here if you don't mind," she told them. She had no desire to see the horrible sight of the mutilated corpses again.

The two agents looked at one another and the bald man nodded his approval. "That's fine, ma'am. We won't be long."

"Okay, just tell me when you're done," she said, relieved they wouldn't make her go with them.

The two agents disappeared down the hallway and out of view. She wondered what they'd think when they found the bloody bodies in the closet.

Their first impression might be to blame her and Weston as the most likely suspects. They would subject them to hours of relentless questioning about where they've been and who they might have spoken with, and would probably conclude they were crazy.

Catherine's heart beat faster as she realized that she and Weston could be blamed for the murder. By the time the mess was worked out she would be in debt with legal fees or worse, in prison for a crime she didn't commit.

She had to come up with a lie about the bodies. And if the police began to dig, there was also the question of the murdered teens close to her house. She could feel beads of sweat run down her armpits as she realized how truly deep she was in trouble.

Now, as she waited for the two agents, she wished she'd never called them. She should've called Weston instead; they could've handled this together, maybe disposed of the bodies somehow and forgotten it had ever happened.

She was pulled from her thoughts to find Agent Adare suddenly at her side, his face empty of emotion.

Catherine gasped. "Oh, sorry 'bout that, you startled me."

"We couldn't find any sign of the bodies you reported, ma'am. There's no blood and nothing looks out of place"

She swallowed the lump in her throat in shock and said, "What? But I don't understand..."

"There are no bodies in the hall closet or writing on the bathroom mirror. We couldn't find anything." She saw he didn't look pleased.

Catherine shoved past him. "That's ridiculous, of course they're here. I saw them plain as day. Hell, I stepped in the blood," she said and went to the closet where the other agent was standing with his arms crossed, also looking very unhappy.

She peered into the closet, her mind already telling her what she would find when she gasped to see it was empty. No dangling bodies, nothing.

She slumped to her knees, not understanding what was happening. "They were here. I saw them," she whispered.

"Ma'am, are you aware that filing a false police report is a crime and you can be fined or worse, you can spend up to thirty days in jail?" the blond agent asked as he walked up behind her. He helped her to her feet.

"But I'm telling you they were there. There was blood on the floor." She looked down to see the floor was clean.

She turned and went to the bathroom, leaving the agents in the hallway. All she saw was her face staring back at her in the polished mirror. No words were written on the clear surface, no elongated handprint.

She might have stared at herself forever if she wasn't snapped out of it by the sound of the front door closing.

Catherine spun around and raced for the door. The two agents were gone. She ran into the main hall of the building and to the front entrance that led to the street.

Once there, she saw the two agents stuffing three black body bags into the back of the Sedan.

"Hey, wait, what are you doing?" She locked eyes with Agent Adare.

"We're doing our job, ma'am," he answered coldly. "Now listen closely. You didn't see anything, you were mistaken. It was a prank someone was playing on you." Before she could reply, the man opened the passenger door and slid inside, closing the door and blocking Catherine's view thanks to the tinted windows.

The other agent was already in the driver's seat, and no sooner did his door close, then the Sedan pulled away from the curb to be lost in traffic.

Catherine tried to read the license plate, but she couldn't make it out before another car blocked her view.

"Son-of-a-bitch," she cursed, and ran back inside the apartment building. She snatched her car keys and her cell phone from the small end table in the living room, then took the shotgun and the duffel bag it was in, wanting it with her just in case.

Barely closing the apartment door behind her, she dashed out of the apartment and to her car in the back parking lot. A few people out and about watched her run by, wondering why she was in such a rush.

She jumped behind the wheel of her car, drove out of the parking lot, and was in traffic less than two minutes after the Sedan had pulled away from the curb.

Her one hope was that the Sedan wasn't in a rush and she could catch up to it.

She gambled that the main street was one long thoroughfare for over three miles and that if she was lucky, she might catch up to the Sedan; especially as there was a traffic light at every intersection.

For every traffic light she got a red one on, she drove through it to the sound of honking horns and screaming, irate drivers. One driver flipped her off and she almost thought he was going to follow her before he turned at the next corner.

She ignored them all, knowing it was the only way to make up the time she'd lost getting to her car.

"I'm gonna find you bastards," she said to herself as she swerved through another red light, almost causing a three car pileup. "And when I do, you're going to give me some answers."

CHAPTER FIFTEEN

Weston checked his watch to see it was eleven twenty. He had forty minutes to get to the Miles warehouse and meet with the Watcher. A chill went down his back as he recalled the strange humanoid's startling blue eyes and placid demeanor.

The Greys hadn't hurt him yet, but that didn't necessarily mean they wouldn't do so now or in the future.

Weston wanted to proceed cautiously yet have some reassurance if things began to look dangerous. In short, he needed a weapon, and fast.

He had a small pocket knife on him. He used it in the book store to open boxes of books but the blade was dulled from years of use. He needed a gun and the shotgun was still back at his apartment, and even if he wanted to get it, the shotgun wasn't exactly a weapon he could conceal. He needed something small, like a handgun.

As he punched out for the day an idea formed in his mind instantly. After he was robbed five years ago, Blake began keeping a loaded .357 Colt Python under the cash register. Weston had never asked the man where he'd gotten the gun but he'd seen it plenty of times when he worked the counter.

Weston had just started working at the book store and had heard the story the next day. Blake was about to close the book store for the night when two men carrying crowbars threatened to beat his head in unless Blake gave them all the money in the register. Blake complied, called the police after the thieves left, and installed a security camera the next day.

Probably assuming Blake was an easy target, the same two men made a return visit a year later but Blake pulled out the .357 and held the two robbers hostage until the police arrived. Blake was praised as a local hero and the event even made the newspapers. He'd kept the gun under the counter ever since, taking it out every few months for target practice and cleaning. For his own protection, Weston needed that gun now. If he could just get Blake away from the register long enough, he could borrow the handgun and return it in the morning without Blake noticing.

Weston strolled out of the back room and quickly came up with a diversion. "Hey, Blake, I just finished, but there's a problem."

Blake looked up at him from the book he was reading.

"What seems to be the trouble, Weston?"

"I couldn't find a couple of books in the computer and I think I might've put the wrong price on them. Could you help me check to make sure I got it right?"

"I trust your judgment. Don't worry about it," Blake said in an annoyed, firm tone.

"But if I messed up it might piss off a customer who'll feel we tried to screw them," Weston said, willing the man to leave the register for a few seconds.

Instead of rushing to the back room to check, Blake stood his ground and said one of the kindest things Weston had ever heard him utter. "Weston, you've worked here for almost six years and you pretty much never make a mistake. Go to wherever you're going, and don't worry about it."

Weston wanted to do just that but he knew he needed that gun. It would be his only protection if his meeting wasn't as altruistic as he hoped. Instead of leaving, he remained standing still.

"What's wrong? Is something the matter?" Blake asked from the counter.

"I..." Weston lowered his head as he tried to decide on another ruse. But when he checked his watch, he saw he didn't have a lot of time left to make the meeting. That made up his mind for him, and though he knew he was taking a risk, he decided he would have to be honest with Blake and see where it took him.

"Blake, listen, I can't really explain why, but I need to borrow the .357 today."

For a moment, Blake's eyes widened and he reached under the cash register and withdrew the large handgun, setting it on the counter top.

"It's about that message you got, isn't it?"

"Yeah, it is," Weston agreed.

"What kind of trouble are you in?" Blake whispered, even though the store was devoid of customers.

"No trouble, I just need some protection. The man I'm meeting is dangerous and it wouldn't hurt to know I can defend myself."

Blake nodded. "I understand," he said. "You don't trust him. I don't either, I could see that the second I saw him come into the store. All right, come with me to the office and I'll fit you with a holster and some extra bullets."

Blake locked the front door of the book store and put the **Be Back in Five** sign on the door, then he led the way to the small office in the rear of the book store. There were windows and a small desk, the office basically a small storage room that had been modified. He gestured for Weston to have a seat on the lone chair besides the desk and chair he used as he unlocked the top drawer of the desk.

"I keep extra ammunition back here in case of emergencies," Blake said as he placed a black gun holster on the desk and followed it with a handful of bullets.

"As you know, I keep this gun for protection. You do remember the robbery, don't you?"

Weston smirked as he imagined the look on the criminals' faces when Blake pulled out and pointed the .357 at them. "Yeah, I remember."

"Okay, then, let's get you set up so you can leave."

Blake took the gun holster and fit one loop around Weston's arm, then drew the strap along his waist and connected it with a snap buckle.

"How does that feel?" Blake asked.

Weston moved his arm up and down, getting the feel for the shoulder holster. "It feels good."

"You'll need to wear a jacket over it to hide it. I have one you can borrow," Blake said, as he handed him the gun and some extra bullets for it. "Let's hope you don't need all of them."

Weston nodded, agreeing completely. "I don't know how to thank you for this, Blake."

"It's no problem. What else are bosses for?" He laughed a little, but it came out as more of a snort. Blake pulled out another handgun from the drawer and showed it to Weston. "And this one is a Desert Eagle. You can hide it around your calf for emergencies."

"How do I wear it?"

Blake produced another gun holster. This one was smaller, but functioned in the same capacity as the other. He lifted Weston's right pant leg and hooked the gun holster up to his calf. He put the Desert Eagle into place, and lowered the pant leg.

"Walk a few steps and see if it stays in place," he instructed.

Weston rose from the seat, stepped out of the room, walked a few steps, and returned. "I can feel it there, but I can walk fine."

"Good, now you're all set," Blake grinned. "Let me get you that coat so you can go."

Weston followed him to the front of the store. Blake took a black coat from a hook and gave it to him. Weston vaguely remembered seeing the coat hanging on the peg before. It was lightweight, perfect for the cool but not yet cold weather. He put it on and saw it was almost a perfect fit.

"Thanks again, Blake. I won't forget this."

"Now don't lose anything and I expect to see you in here the first thing tomorrow morning."

"Don't worry, I'll be here."

Weston placed the gun into the shoulder holster and zipped up the coat.

"You take care of yourself now," Blake said, as though Weston was taking an extended lunch break and not heading to a private meeting with two guns strapped to his person.

Weston waved and left the book store. The .357's weight was reassuring against his side. He walked down the street with a new confidence, knowing if he ran into trouble he could protect himself.

Blake had given him the gun without any qualms or questions at all and he realized that no matter how much you thought you knew someone, they could always surprise you.

He recalled the way the Watcher had reacted to the shotgun he brought along last time they'd met. Then, the weapon had been in full view. Now, he would look harmless, weak, and if the Watcher tried anything, the mysterious figure was in for a very unpleasant surprise.

He stuffed his hands into the jacket, feeling the weight of the Desert Eagle on his leg. The Watcher had played enough games with him; now it was time for Weston to play one of his own.

* * *

Catherine could see the black Sedan up ahead. She was gaining ground at each traffic light she sped through, and getting closer to the answers she craved. When she first saw the men in the black suits, she thought their choice of outfit seemed odd, but now, as she chased after them, she realized who they really were.

"The men in black," she hissed through her teeth. They were the mysterious G-men who would appear and make a UFO sighting disappear.

They must have intercepted her call to the police and had arrived instead. She wouldn't be surprised if something she had said on the phone was a flagged word they monitored.

But they had simply entered Weston's apartment, stole the evidence, and fled. They hadn't touched her which was odd. Normally, she would have had been silenced. So for some reason they weren't afraid of what she knew, probably because if she tried to tell someone, she would only end up being locked up as insane.

The black Sedan ahead suddenly slowed and came to a stop at a red light, but when the light turned green, it didn't go.

The Sedan didn't move, and she wondered what they were up to. They were in the heart of the Old City, and traffic began building up behind them as horns blared and angry drivers cursed.

Catherine resisted the urge to exit her car run over to them, but she learned her lesson from the last time she addressed a group of strangers in a car, and decided it was best to wait them out and see what they were going to do next.

As she watched, the passenger window of the Sedan opened and the blond agent popped out, now facing her. In his hand, he held a gun which he aimed at her windshield.

Catherine ducked and screamed.

A bullet punched through the glass and pounded into the seat where her head was only a second ago.

In a panic, Catherine eased her foot off the brake pedal. Her car rammed into the car in front of her as screams filled the street and people ran for their lives.

Her car was struck from behind by a scared driver and the horrible sound of metal connecting against metal shrieked in her ears. She was jolted against the dashboard in the collision and didn't move for fear they would shoot again.

Tires squealed and the Sedan sped away, running a red light and causing a Lincoln Town Car to swerve and crash into a storefront, sending glass shards flying in every direction.

People began to scream and an alarm sounded from inside the store.

Catherine sat up. She could smell burned rubber and exhaust seeping through the hole in her windshield. The hole was small, and she felt the temptation to reach up and poke her index finger though it.

Their message was very clear to her. If she continued to chase after them, they would kill her. With trembling hands, she gripped the steering wheel and swung out of traffic. The driver behind her was yelling at her to stop, but she ignored him, stepping on the gas pedal and surging forward.

There was no time to worry about such petty things as insurance claims. In the background, she could hear the wail of police sirens and she knew someone had called them.

She needed to get to Weston, tell him what was going on and make sure he was okay.

With the wind whistling through the hole in her windshield, she continued down the street, her resolve still firm.

CHAPTER SIXTEEN

Weston parked three blocks away from his destination and walked the rest of the way. He picked a busy parking lot next door to an Italian restaurant. If he never returned, the police would eventually run his license plate to see who his car belonged to and report him missing. He left a note for Catherine on the driver's seat saying he was sorry that he trusted the Watcher and failed to save her. But in his heart, he knew differently, he wouldn't fail her. Whatever the Watcher wanted, this would be the last time. He would get the answers he needed so both he and Catherine could go on with their lives.

"Okay, let's do this," Weston said to himself as he looked into his own eyes by way of the rearview mirror.

He stepped out of the vehicle, locked the car, and began walking to the warehouse. Questions about the Grey's intentions raced through his mind. In their last meeting, he had given the being the DVD it had wanted, and it had probed his mind as well as sending images into his. He wasn't looking forward to a second encounter, but he knew this was something that had to be done.

The Colt Python bounced against his side, letting him know he wasn't helpless if it came to a fight. He didn't know what a bullet would do to a Grey, but he had a feeling it would be like shooting any meat-based being.

The warehouse loomed before him, dark and decayed. The area surrounding the building was abandoned, as if there was an unspoken word to stay clear. It looked like one or two of the structures had seen fire recently, the facades blackened and scorched, and he wondered if it had been arson or just teenagers having fun.

Weston approached the entrance to the warehouse with caution. He peered into a cracked and dirty window and saw a couple of dusty tables and leftover machinery. The warehouse was devoid of life, but he knew better. He could sense he wasn't alone, the feeling like an electric shock running down his spine. Perhaps it was a residue of touching minds with the being. As he inspected the warehouse a little more, he saw why the meeting had been placed here. No one would be around to get in the way as there was nothing of value or business operating in the vicinity.

Weston tried the rusted front door to the building and was more than mildly surprised when it opened on old creaking hinges. He entered the warehouse. The daylight was immediately swallowed by darkness, shadows hiding in the corners of the large room in wreaths of blackness. He advanced, moving around the tables and metal shelves, kicking aside the detritus of beer cans and empty condom wrappers, the remnants of a thousands teenage parties.

"Hello, are you here?" he called out, his voice echoing across the walls and making him shiver despite himself. His voice sounded small in the large interior of the warehouse, and he swallowed, his mouth now dry.

A glass beer bottle rolled on the floor ahead of him until it stopped by hitting a table leg. The sound echoed for a moment and went silent.

Weston paused as suddenly images of violence flowed into his mind like an old reel of film: Vietnam soldiers shooting villagers with high-powered machine guns, then teenagers hiding pistols in backpacks to enter schools, gangs firing at each other from sport cars, and finally, an image of a bank robber shooting at the police as he stole money from a bank.

Weston shook the images away and replaced them with thoughts of his own—of peace. Visions of singing in church, having dinner with old friends, a family playing on the beach and another of a birthday party, and a small child blowing out candles as family and friends laughed and clapped rushed through his mind.

"But you do not come to me in peace," the Watcher spoke in his mind. "You have come armed."

"I came prepared," Weston said. "Why are you hiding?"

The overhead lights flickered to life.

Weston blinked his eyes as he saw small white lights. Slowly they receded and his vision was clear once more. Before him was the large expanse of the warehouse. The shadows were now banished and he saw the interior was crammed with broken tables and stacks of twisted machinery heaped in piles along the walls. He walked among the trash, careful not to step on anything hazardous.

"I've never harmed you," the Watcher said. "Why do you arm yourself now? Are you afraid of me?"

Weston stumbled over a chunk of metal from an unknown piece of machinery. He steadied himself and examined his surroundings more thoroughly. Although the lights were on, the left side of the warehouse was still shrouded in darkness. He maneuvered past a dismembered table and nearly tripped on the wooden arms of a chair littering the floor.

"Where are you?"

"Would you shoot me if you knew?" the Watcher asked.

"No, of course not. I'm just being cautious, anybody would be. I won't shoot you if you don't try and hurt me," Weston promised. He opened his coat and withdrew the .357.

The lights flicked off immediately, casting the darkness across the warehouse once more.

"Wait, wait just a minute."

Weston placed the gun on the floor. "There, see, I'm unarmed," he explained.

There was movement in front of him like a gust of wind had shot past.

He could see a tall shape form out of the darkness and draw near. The Grey didn't adhere to the long trench coat or dark sunglasses this time. He was wearing a tight fitting spandex, the color matching his skin.

"You're frightened of me," it said.

Weston could barely move his lips as two blue, oval eyes formed around taunt grey skin.

"Yes, I suppose I am."

"You have no need to be afraid of me. I do not intend you harm. We can help each other," the Grey said. "But you have to do as I say."

The Grey stared down at him, boring into his mind, telling him what to do.

A thousand images flashed through Weston's head. Visions of the emptiness of outer space, a triangle shaped ship, Earth, blue light streaming into windows, people...hundreds of people: men, women, children of all races, ages, and background were snatched from their homes, taken, experimented on, and then returned no worse for wear, almost none of them knowing it had happened, believing it nothing but a bad dream.

More images blurred together: another triangular spacecraft, this one darker and made of organic material, kidnapping humans, mutilating them beyond recognition, draining them, and dumping their lifeless carcasses wherever they pleased.

"Stop it!" Weston yelled as he gripped the sides of his head. It felt like his skull was ready to burst. "Please, stop."

The images faded, a million screaming voices blending together to then vanish.

Weston's shirt was drenched in sweat as his consciousness returned to normal. He gasped as he tried to gain control of himself once more. "Who are they? What do they want from us? Why did they do that to all those people?"

The Grey placed its long, tapered fingers onto Weston's shoulder and to him they felt spongy, like a squid's, yet when flexed they became ridged and hard.

"Come with me," the Grey said, and led Weston through the darkness towards the back of the warehouse. "I brought you here to witness and remember."

Weston hesitated as he followed, not wanting to trip and perhaps crack his head open on an errant piece of stray machinery. He remembered the piles of junk blocking the path to where the being was taking him.

"Why have you stopped?"

"I can't see," Weston said.

"Don't you trust me?"

Weston thought back to the .357 he'd left on the floor. If the Grey wanted to, it could do whatever it wanted and Weston wouldn't stand a chance. The being didn't know about the Desert Eagle on his ankle and he made sure not to think about it, knowing the Grey could read his thoughts.

"You need to understand something," Weston said. "It's not a great feeling not having the upper hand. People are taught all their lives not to trust strangers and whether it's right or wrong we fear things we don't understand. It's just our nature. That's why we have so many wars on my planet."

"I am no stranger to you, Weston. Look into your past; we have met before, although you may refuse to remember it."

Weston had no memory of the tall grey humanoid, but he did recall a nightmare that had haunted him in his youth. He was five years old and awoke in the middle of the night. Someone was in his bedroom watching over him. He called the tall visitor the Watcher, but he couldn't remember anything else. He had always believed it had just been a dream.

"You will in time," the Grey replied. "Now, follow me, time is short." The Grey stretched out an arm, the fingers of the hand open, palm up.

Weston took the offered hand and clasped it tightly. An electric current surged through him; it was an unpleasant sensation but one he could tolerate.

The Grey led him through the darkness.

It was as if the Grey could see in the dark as it led Weston around the obstructions blocking their path.

The air suddenly dropped ten degrees and Weston could just make out the outline of a door ahead.

"Are you taking me to your office?" Weston chuckled, his way of fighting off the growing nervousness he felt.

"No, I am taking you into a freezing chamber where the dark men keep their specimens."

Weston tried to stop then, deciding he didn't want to go in there anymore but he was drawn into the room, as if he was being controlled.

As he stepped inside with the Grey leading the way, the door slammed behind him, and no sooner did the door close, then his freewill returned.

"Why are you doing this? I gave you what you wanted, I gave you the DVD," Weston said to the Grey, his breath pluming out before him in the frigid cold. He was trapped in the chamber, and as he looked around in the dark, he saw no way to escape.

"Amusing. Why do you think I wanted the DVD? I am not the one hunting you. I have no concern for alleged evidence brought to the public. I am conducting my own experiments the way members of your race capture animals, study them, and let them go." The Grey pressed close enough that Weston could feel an intense vibration radiating from the figure's skin. "The 'dark men' as you call them are not men at all. They are the opposite of my kind and will stop at nothing until the harvest is completed. You, your woman, Catherine, and the rest of the worlds' population are in grave danger. You must realize this by now."

Weston backed away from the Grey until he touched the door. His hands were numb from the cold and he shoved them into his pockets to keep them warm.

"What is this harvest exactly? Why is it so important?"

The lights in the chamber's ceiling snapped on and Weston saw he was in a large meat freezer. He gasped in shock, unable to believe his eyes at the tableaux before him. He would've screamed if his mouth could move, but he found himself retreating back into his mind, into the far corners of his head where scenes like the one before him didn't exist in reality. He felt paralyzed as he took in the charnel house of death, wishing he could close his eyes and make it all go away, like a bad dream.

Racks of dead human bodies hung from hooks like laundered clothing at the dry cleaners. At least a hundred men and women stared at him with sightless, cored-out eyes, and most of the skin on the bodies was missing.

"This is the harvest, Weston. This is their work." The Grey wrapped his arm around Weston and forced him to get a closer look at the bodies. Weston stared at the gaping holes in the bellies of the women, and missing genitals of the men.

As he fought the urge to vomit, he struggled to break free of the Grey's grasp. He wanted out. He didn't want to see this. He didn't want to know anything about it.

He was only one man. What could he do about this?

But the Grey held on to him tightly, curling its long fingers around his back, and urging him to stay with the power of its mind.

"We're being slaughtered like cattle," Weston gasped as he leaned over and sucked in a breath of air, closing his eyes until the nausea had passed.

"No, it is more than that, so much more," the Grey said. It made him stand a few inches away from the dismembered corpse of a young man. He looked to be in his early twenties when he died. He had been handsome and full of promise, but now, he was just another dead body swinging from a meat hook in an abandoned building.

"Your government knows about this, Weston, but they cover it up. They cannot go public because if they did, all it would accomplish is to frighten the population. They have no defense against the dark men or us for that matter. They estimate the losses every year and crush every shred of evidence they can get their hands on, but accept it as something they cannot control."

"Take me out of here, please. I don't want to see this anymore," Weston begged.

"But you must see it, you must understand. You can bring them down, Weston. You and Catherine together can stop this madness."

"How can we possibly do that?"

"We need to…" The Watcher paused and jerked his large head toward the door.

"What is it?" he asked.

"They have returned. We must go," the Grey said.

Before Weston could respond, the Watcher was leading him through the now opened freezer door. The warehouse lights were on but the warehouse was empty. The Watcher moved so fast Weston couldn't comprehend the movements as he ran behind the running figure. One second they were outside the freezer, the next, they had reached the center of the warehouse. Weston was breathing hard from the dash but the Grey seemed fine, as if exertion was nothing to it.

Then the main entrance door swung open at the front of the warehouse and four tall, dark-eyed Greys in trench coats and hats charged inside.

"We're too late," the Watcher said. "I want you to take this and run." He picked up a briefcase hidden under some debris, throwing the junk aside, and forced it into Weston's hands.

"What's this? Where did you get this?"

"I hid it before you arrived. There is no time to explain further."

The four Greys disregarded their clothing and stood in a line. If they were angry at Weston and the Watcher's intrusion they didn't show it. Expressionless, they withdrew long knives from their belts and sped forward in a blur of motion.

Weston had no time to move before they reached him; the figures moving faster than a human would have been able to. Black eyes held him immobile and paralyzed his body.

A long shimmering blade was raised and brought down towards his belly and Weston screamed, but the knife didn't puncture him. Before the knife struck him, the Watcher moved in front of him, blocking the knife and striking back with a long golden needle. The needle slammed into the attacking Grey's head, sending it to the floor, either dead or unconscious, Weston couldn't tell.

Weston tried to run then but two more Greys took the fallen one's place and this time the Watcher wasn't in time to save him. A pain like liquid fire sliced through Weston's chest, quickly followed by another across his thigh.

He felt skin and muscle part, exposing the bone beneath as he fell to the floor, screaming in agony. The two Greys loomed over him, staring at him as he came apart like a worn rag doll with the stitches severed.

The Watcher reached for him, grabbed his arm, and pulled, dragging him away from the melee. Weston slid across the floor and crashed into a lopsided table. His blood leaked out of the knife wounds and pooled around him as he fought to remain conscious. The Watcher was a blur of motion, and it struck the two black-eyed Greys with the shimmering needle. Once the long needle was embedded into their oval heads, they ceased attacking and stared slumped to the floor, their oval eyes seeing things that only they could fathom.

The Watcher bent over Weston and placed a black object on his chest. The pain became immense, a thousand fold what he was already feeling and he knew he would black out at any moment. His chest was burning and the fire spread down his belly, through his limbs, and to his head, suffusing his entire body.

"Take it off!" Weston screamed. "For Christ's sake, take it off, you're killing me!"

The Watcher waved his hand over Weston's eyes and the burning sensations faded. When the object was withdrawn from his chest, he was able to see it better. The device was black and organic; it reminded him of a slug, until he saw the sharp protrusion sticking up from its center.

"You must get up," the Watcher demanded.

Weston surveyed his body, the wounds he'd suffered were now gone; there were no marks where the knives had separated his flesh, only the slight hint of red where the wounds had been sealed.

"How did you do that?" he gasped as he touched himself. His clothing was torn and bloody from the blades but the flesh beneath was unmarred. It was hard to believe it was true.

The Watcher helped him to his feet and then retrieved the briefcase from the floor. "There is no time; you need to leave, now."

The dark beings wobbled to their feet. They were recovering and were lining up together once more to renew their attack. The Watcher ushered Weston past them and brought him to the exit. He hesitated as he stared at the humanoids.

Weston pried the door open. "Come on! Let's get the hell out of here!"

The Watcher didn't respond. Weston watched as the Grey seemed to sway on its feet and then slump to its knees.

"What are you doing? Get up," Weston urged, but quickly realized what had happened.

A sharp blade had appeared in the middle of the Watcher's sternum, as if by magic. Weston stared in horror as the blade began to move, sliding downward.

He found himself staring into two fist-sized eyes the color of midnight as the enemy Grey peered over the Watcher's shoulder.

The Grey had snuck up behind the Watcher and had stabbed it in the back, now using the blade to slice its prey in half.

As Weston raced out of the door and onto the street, he could feel tendrils of the attacking Grey's minds as they systematically attempted to bore into his brain for information. At first, the sensation was unbearable and nearly caused him to tumble over and wither in agony. But the further he moved from the warehouse and the alien figures inside, the better he felt.

The link the dark beings were attempting to establish was soon broken and Weston didn't know what they were trying to accomplish but he knew it couldn't be good. He fled, dashing across the empty lot and running past the dilapidated buildings. Everything had happened so quickly. One minute the Watcher was telling him about the harvest and the next they were fighting the four dark Greys.

Where am I running to? he asked himself as he jogged through the pedestrians on the sidewalk, oblivious to the ordeal Weston had just experienced.

He didn't know where he was running to, all he wanted was to escape, to keep going until he was somewhere they couldn't reach him.

Reality had shifted on him once more, altering and showing its teeth. Life wasn't as it seemed, the darkness of outer space held more than stars and planets, a sinister enemy had come to Earth, and it was bent on destroying it. Flashes of the mutilated bodies he'd seen hanging in the freezer at the warehouse blinded his vision. The people he shoved past suddenly become naked and dangled from hooks impaled in their necks. They were nothing but hollowed-out shells of humanity, each staring at him with sightless eyes.

He was out of breath and his lungs struggled for more oxygen. His legs throbbed with an intense stabbing pain and he was losing his perspective. The street he stood on vanished as two black eyes appeared in the sky, hovering over him to swallow him whole.

"This isn't happening. This isn't real."

He collapsed on the pavement, the briefcase clattering beside him. The Greys had penetrated his mind, flooding it with false realities, and making him helpless to stop them. They would let him wait on the streets, the people around him unaware about what was occurring, until they came to get him. As people walked by him, wondering what was wrong with the man, wondering if he was either crazy or drunk, Weston thrashed in the invisible bonds holding him in place, but he couldn't break free.

He had lost.

"Weston, oh my God, no..."

Catherine's voice penetrated his stupor a little, and he looked up to see her coming towards him, shoving past others who were gawking at the weird man on the sidewalk; her face was filled with worry for him.

"What are you doing out here?" she asked as she knelt down beside him, cupping his head in her hands.

Weston couldn't answer her. He could see her face, but the large eyes in the sky continued to press in on him.

Catherine lifted him to his feet and helped him to her car at the end of the street.

The watchful eyes faded before Weston's vision as he put even more distance from him and the warehouse. With each yard he traversed, the street slowly began to return to normal.

As he came back to himself, he saw Catherine was by his side.

"We have to get out of here," Weston gasped, his head a massive migraine from the Greys' intrusion. "They're coming for me."

She helped him inside her car, took the briefcase from him, and tossed it into the backseat. With Weston in the vehicle, she slammed his door and ran around to the driver's side. She climbed behind the steering wheel and pulled into traffic, her eyes trying to look everywhere at once. She had been angry for losing the black Sedan, but she had found Weston who looked like he'd been through a war and lost. As she reached over and checked his bloody clothes, she was relieved to see he wasn't wounded. The blood must be from someone else, she figured.

With Weston slumped over in the passenger seat, unconscious, she concentrated on driving.

CHAPTER SEVENTEEN

When Catherine pulled into Sera Market it was near dark. This was her second stop before going to the cabin, her first was to work. The funeral home was a good fifteen miles out of the way, but well worth the trip.

Upon entering, she informed the funeral director that she needed to use her vacation days immediately. She made up a story of a family emergency, and she was able to get a week off.

Before leaving, she went to the embalming room to gather some supplies. She took an array of chemicals and scalpels, shoving them into a black bag found in a storage closet. She didn't know what she might need, so she grabbed anything that looked useful.

When she returned to the car, Weston was still unconscious. After checking him to see he was now sleeping, she kissed his cheek and then drove back to the cabin in the mountains, realizing she had been foolish to leave in the first place.

Her great plan she had told Weston she had was all for nothing. After seeing the bodies hanging in the closet, she realized she was in way over her head.

The cabin was the safest place she could think of to go with it being secluded; at least they would see an enemy coming.

And if the Greys did try to get to them, this time she would be prepared, and this time she would get more proof than a home movie. This time she would get a Grey corpse.

She shook Weston gently after she parked at Sera Market. He didn't respond to her, just moaned in his sleep. She withdrew the black bag she'd taken from the funeral home, opened it, and dug around. She quickly found a small vial in a zip lock bag. The vial was used for reviving people who'd fainted while in the presence of the deceased, usually when a loved one saw a body before the funeral to make sure they were pleased with the cadaver's clothes, hair and preparation that went into preparing a body for viewing by family and friends.

The capsule was to be placed under the nostrils of the unconscious person and then broken. Catherine had used the method once before on an elderly woman who collapsed during her husband's funeral. She never forgot the horrible smell released after the capsule was broken in half, she could only relate the smell to ammonia or rotten eggs.

She placed the white capsule under Weston's nose and broke the seal. An arid fragrance spilled from the vial, releasing a chemical strong enough to wake the dead. Weston groaned and moved his head away from the pungent aroma.

"God, what the hell is that smell?" he said, his voice groggy.

Catherine rolled down the windows and tossed out the remains of the capsule.

"Good, you're awake," she said as she touched his cheek lovingly. "I didn't want you sleeping any longer in case you had a concussion."

"Where are we?" he asked as he sat up, wiping drool from the corner of his mouth with the back of his sleeve.

"Near the mountains. We're at a grocery store. Are you thirsty or hungry?"

"I could go for a sandwich," Weston said, and pressed his palms to the side of his head. "And yeah, come to think of it, my mouth is as dry as the Sahara."

"You all right?"

"Yeah, I'll live, I guess. I just have one hell of a headache." He sucked in a breath of air and let it out, looking around for the first time since waking up. The car was in a small parking lot, and there was a small grocery store to his right. A few other cars were in the parking lot as well, but it was basically quiet. "What happened to me?"

"I found you lying on the sidewalk downtown. You were screaming."

"How did you find me?"

"Dumb luck actually. I was following a black Sedan, the story to that I'll tell you on the drive to the cabin. I lost the sedan but found you instead."

"Seems like a hell of a coincidence," he said as he opened his door and placed his feet on the pavement. He was woozy and didn't want to get up just yet.

"Yeah, I thought the same thing at first. But haven't you notice how nothing has been a coincidence. I found you because the sedan I was chasing was headed the same way as you were." she frowned. "And I thought you were at work, what were you doing there, anyway?"

"I'll tell you my story after you tell me yours, deal?"

"Fine," she said as she stepped out of the car and closed her door. "I'm going into get some supplies. I'll be right back."

Weston got out of the car, too. "Wait, I'll go in with you."

"Are you sure?" she asked. She went over to him and stood beside him, as he didn't look that surefooted at the moment.

He nodded. "Yeah, I need to stretch my legs anyway. I'm sore all over." He made a disgusted face. "What was that stuff you stuck under my nose anyway?"

"I got it from work. It's for people who faint, like smelling salt. You've been unconscious for almost two hours, Weston."

"Two hours..." His gaze drifted out to the mountains on the horizon. "The Watcher, we were in a warehouse. He... died."

"No, not here," she hushed him. "We'll talk about it later when we're alone in the car." She watched a mother and child pushing a carriage full of groceries. As they passed her, she smiled and the mother grinned back politely. Catherine shook her head as she watched the mother reach her car and let the child inside.

They have no idea what was really going on in the world, she thought. How one second your world was fine and then the next everything was upside down.

"We can't trust anyone, Weston. We can only trust each other. We need some more supplies if we're going to stay up at the cabin longer than before. Why don't you wait here and I'll go get them?" She handed him the keys and he took them in his left hand. "If you want, keep the engine running, just in case we need to get out of here fast," she said, and headed for the grocery store.

He may not like it that we had to stop here but we need more food and I wouldn't mind having a few more surprises for the enemy when they show up.

Weston watched her go and leaned against the car and tried to relax. Once more he checked where he should have wounds and was still shocked to see his skin was fine. Even the redness had disappeared.

He reached down to his ankle where the gun Blake had given him should be but his ankle was empty. Sometime during his escape it had fallen off. He had lost both of the guns Blake had given him. The next time he saw his boss he wasn't looking forward to telling him that.

He studied the few cars in the parking lot but nothing was happening to cause him alarm and he was just calming down when a car pulled into the lot. Weston's eyes went wide when he saw it was the Buick. Catherine had just gone inside and there was no time to get her. His heart was pounding as adrenaline suffused his system and he spotted the shotgun on the backseat of the car. He reached inside, about to grab it and blow the dark Greys back to where they came from, when the Buick parked near the main entrance to the grocery store and an old lady with a wooden cane stepped out. She was over seventy with thinning white hair and a flowered dress. No one else was in the car.

He quickly realized the Buick before him wasn't the one the Greys drove. It was just another Buick and this one was dark blue, not black.

He let go of the shotgun and let out a massive sigh of relief. What were the odds? Pretty good actually. Buicks were common, even the older ones.

He laughed to himself as he crossed his hands over his chest, telling himself he was now officially crazy, jumping at every shadow he saw.

Catherine pushed a shopping cart through the aisles, going straight to the deli first. She picked out a large turkey sandwich for Weston and a tuna salad for herself, then, a gallon of 1% milk, crackers, cheese, bread, and a few cans of refried beans. Her last stop was at the automotive section. She found what she was looking for right away, three bottles of oil and four spray cans of carburetor cleaner.

She added a handful of cigarette lighters and a box of wooden matches on her way to checkout. The cashier, a seventeen year old girl, at the register gave her a friendly smile and proceeded to ring up her groceries, sometimes looking curiously at the odd assortment of items, but knowing better than to say anything. What a customer purchased was none of her business and she knew some of the tourists that came through were a little weird.

Everything was going smoothly until the power went out, drowning the interior of the store in darkness.

Catherine's vision was thrown into total blackness. Blinded, she remained steadfast and gripped the counter for support. Was this an attack by the Greys? And if so, why were they being so brazen with so many witnesses?

A loud voice suddenly cut through the darkness. "Everyone stay calm and stay where you are! There's no need to panic!"

Catherine witnessed a flash of light shine through the glass storefront. *No, I'm not ready, not here! Where's Weston? Oh, God, they got Weston!* she thought as she ducked under the counter and began searching for something she could use as a weapon.

Her hand wrapped around a broom handle used when the cashier was cleaning up and she pulled it to her, her eyes darting back and forth as her heart beat fast within her chest. If they were going to take her, they wouldn't get her without a fight.

The lights suddenly flickered and popped back on again, taking the store out of the primeval darkness.

"It's fine folks, we blew a fuse, sorry for the inconvenience," the voice called out once more as he put away the large flashlight he'd been carrying for just such an emergency. The cashier peered over the register to look down at Catherine, a curious look on her face.

Catherine stared up at the girl, and then stood up, using the counter to steady herself as she dropped the broom handle back to the floor.

"Sorry, I was a little spooked I guess."

The cashier shrugged, "It happens."

"How much do I owe you?"

"Forty-two bucks even."

Catherine paid, and with a half smile and a look of embarrassment, she left the store.

"Tourists," the cashier said as she watched Catherine leave. "They get weirder every year."

* * *

The road to the cabin was a lonely stretch of concrete surrounded by an endless cloud of towering trees.

With night having fallen, Catherine searched the skies for a pulsating blue light or a Buick tailing their progress, but she saw neither. The skies were dark, and she hadn't seen another vehicle since leaving the store, which is how it usually was when she drove deep into the mountains to reach the cabin.

Weston snored beside her, a constant reminder that he was back to normal. After they left Sera Market, she filled him in on what had happened at his apartment and the end result of the two men in black.

He then shared his adventure with her and by the time he was done, both were ill at ease.

Instead of things getting easier, they continued to grow more complicated with each passing hour.

For a time they didn't talk, each lost in their private thoughts about what would happen next. Catherine never knew Weston had drifted off to sleep until she began to hear him snore.

The long day's events were catching up to her as well. The bodies in the closet, the writing on the mirror, men in black trying to shoot her, and the weird power failure at the grocery store.

When he had commented on the hole in the windshield—which was now stuffed with a tissue to keep out the howling wind—Catherine had only nodded. He had said how lucky she was and how if anything had happened to her he wouldn't know how to deal with it. They had held hands then, both glad to be back together again.

"What did they do to you in that warehouse?" she asked as she ran her fingers through his hair. When he had told her about how his clothes became bloody, he had glossed over it, as if the memory was too much to bear. She hadn't pressed him on the subject.

Weston continued to sleep, momentarily absent from the world.

Her headlights cut through the darkness, and another hour later she finally reached the cabin. It was dark and empty and didn't look disturbed. The front door was closed as were the two windows she could see.

She rubbed Weston's shoulder. "Hey, it's time to wake up. We're here." She shook him harder and yelped when his hand clamped down over hers. He looked at her for a moment as though she were a stranger, his eyes wide with fear. Then, recognition flooded his face and he released her.

"I'm so sorry, Catherine. For a second I thought you were...well, never mind. I think I was having a nightmare." He rubbed his eyes and sat up.

Catherine patted his lap. "It seems to be going around," she said as she rubbed her hand. "That's some grip you've got. How are you feeling?"

"I feel groggy, like I woke up from an operation," he quivered. "Christ, every bone in my body hurts."

Catherine patted his thigh. "After everything you went through I'm not surprised." She opened her door and stepped out, then went to the trunk and after opening it, began taking out bags of groceries. "I bought a few extra items I think we can use to protect ourselves if they come after us up here," she said and showed him the bottles of motor oil and carburetor cleaner in the backseat.

"What are you gonna do with those?" he asked.

"Let's just say that they'll have some unpleasant surprises to deal with if they try for us again."

CHAPTER EIGHTEEN

Once they were settled inside the cabin, Weston decided to open the briefcase. He placed it on the kitchen table beside the shotgun, sat down, and fiddled with the clasp. The Watcher hadn't told him what lay hidden inside, but did stress the briefcase's importance. Weston remembered the force and venom the Watcher had instilled when it had shoved the briefcase into his hands. The Grey had died for whatever resided within the case and now it was Weston's job to finish what had been started.

"I hope it was all worth it," Weston said to himself as he thought of the Watcher dead on the warehouse floor with the blade in its chest.

Upon opening the briefcase, he saw it contained two small items. One, Weston recognized immediately: it was the DVD they had given the Watcher on Hangover Bridge. The event seemed like it had occurred years ago, but only a few days had elapsed since the event. He took the DVD out and placed it on the table, reminding himself to make more copies and port the video onto the internet.

Once it was on the World Wide Web, then the power over the DVD would be useless and whoever wanted it would be helpless to stop it from being viewed.

The other object in the briefcase was a rectangular piece of metal. He would've discounted the item as junk or scrap metal in his former life, before his knowledge of the Watcher and the Greys. That was a simpler life, a happier life, and one he now missed.

He let out a heavy sigh and slumped his shoulders. He was running out of energy, the stress of the past few days catching up to him. Exhausted, he took the piece of metal out of the briefcase and studied it, wondering what its significance was. When he picked it up, he assumed it would be heavier, but it was as light as a feather. He examined the light-weight metal, turning it over, checking for markings or something that suggested its origin. The shimmering metal offered nothing upon closer inspection.

The Watcher had insisted the briefcase was linked to the Greys' demise, and yet the two items he'd left in Weston's care lacked any real evidence to confirm this. Anyone who watched the DVD would probably claim it was a clever hoax and not the real thing. And as far as the piece of metal was concerned…he squeezed his fingers together, crumpling the piece of metal into a ball, like it was tinfoil. He tossed it on the table, already forgetting about it, when it sprang back into its original form.

"Catherine, come here, holy shit!" he shouted as he rose from his chair, knocking it over in his excitement. Catherine was in the main room and within seconds, she charged into the kitchen to see what was wrong.

"Where are they? Are they here?" she shouted as her eyes darted around the small room.

He raised his hand to calm her. "No, relax, no one's here. Come over here, I want to show you something incredible." He picked up the strange metal from the table and repeated what he did before. Catherine gasped in amazement as the metal landed on the table and unfolded like a sponge folded in half and then let go. "Isn't that incredible?" he asked.

"What is it, some kind of rubber?"

"No, that's the crazy thing. It's metal," he said while smiling.

"Metal, but it's…"

"Yeah, I know. It was in the briefcase along with the DVD."

She picked it up and looked at it. For all purposes it was a piece of metal, yet it moved like rubber. "We need to get this to someone who will listen and believe us. This will go a long way to verifying our story."

"I couldn't agree more," Weston said. He returned the metal to the briefcase, but left the DVD out. "So the Watcher wasn't lying when he said this briefcase was important," Weston said.

"What?" she asked.

"The Watcher, he's the being we met on the bridge. He told me that the government knew all about the Greys and that they covered it up." He saw the quizzical look on her face and explained. "The Watcher is a Grey, too, only different. He was sent here to study us without hurting us, but the others weren't. They're here to destroy us."

Catherine closed her eyes and shook her head. "Wait a second, what are you saying?" she asked. She poured herself a glass of water and drank half of it in a single gulp. "Now you're telling me that there are two different alien races living among us, one is bad, the other good?" She sat down and cradled her head in her hands. "How could nobody know about them? Do they just fly into cities snatching whoever they want and everyone is ignorant? Why don't more people know about them?"

"I think people do. All those reports about alien abductions? That's what happens to people. But no one believes them. They're told they imagined it or are just plain nuts."

"But surely someone in authority would believe one of the stories sooner or later," she said.

"Why?" Weston asked. "Think about it. An individual human being likes to idealize themselves as unique and special. We pride ourselves into believing that we can drive better than anyone else and that everyone on the road doesn't know what they're doing. Take that concept and magnify it ten fold. We're blinded by our own ambition and fallacies, and when we're faced with something powerful and unknown, we shun it, telling ourselves we saw a meteor in the sky or ball lightning, instead of acknowledging the fact that there might be something out there watching us. If I told you tall grey beings with big black eyes were kidnapping people to harvest them for God knows what, you'd think I was crazy, right?"

"If I hadn't seen it for myself, then yes, I'd say you'd lost your hold on reality," she said and sat down. She arched her back and fiddled with the empty glass on the table. "Are you telling me there's no hope in trying to convince the public these things really do happen? That these Greys are real?"

"No, there's hope, but we need proof that's so solid there's no way not to accept it as the truth," he replied. "But the public may not want the truth. Maybe our government has the right idea keeping this undercover. If it's proven that there's life out there in space, then the belief system of millions of people will be destroyed in the blink of an eye. And even if we can prove the Greys are real, what will it accomplish in the end? We'll start a media frenzy and nobody will feel safe in their homes again."

She placed her hand over his. "But it's the right thing to do. The human race has a right to know what's happening. The Greys aren't unstoppable. You said the one you met was killed," Catherine explained. "That means they can die."

Weston gave her a reassuring smile. He took her glass and went to the sink to fill it up again.

"Why do you call him the Watcher?" she asked.

As he sat down, he placed the glass on the table before him and folded his hands around it.

"When I was a boy, I always thought somebody was creeping into my room every night. They would hover over my bed and watch over me. I called him the Watcher because that's what he did, he watched over me. I think the being on the bridge was the same one from my childhood."

Catherine closed her eyes and took a few deep breaths. "Okay, so did this 'Watcher' tell you where he was from?"

"No," he replied, realizing she wasn't dealing well with the fact that he'd known about the Grey all his life or believed he did. "I don't know if they came from outer space or anything as far fetched as that, but he made me feel like they came from somewhere both close *and* far away."

He drank some of his water.

She sighed deeply and said, "I wish I could say I'd be happy when this is all over, but it's never going to end, will it?"

He leaned forward and wrapped his hands around hers. "We'll put an end to them. We just need to have enough evidence to convince the skeptics and make the scientists curious. There's still hope."

Catherine was about to answer when a series of heavy knocks rattled the front door. She jumped from her seat, her eyes darting to the front of the cabin.

"Who the hell could that be?" she said.

"I don't know but if they're not friendly they're gonna regret coming here." He hid the briefcase in the hallway closet and grabbed the shotgun, making sure it was loaded and ready. The door shook as an even louder knock than before pounded on the wood.

Weston crossed the cabin and placed his hand on the door-knob, his other on the shotgun.

"Be careful," Catherine warned from the opening to the kitchen.

He nodded and peered out the small window in the door, about head height.

"I don't see anyone out there," he told her.

The door shook again and the sound of knuckles striking wood made him jump.

"Don't answer it," Catherine ordered. "They're trying to trick us."

"I doubt that. If it's them I doubt they would bother knocking. I'm just gonna take a quick peek." He pointed to the closet. "Go get the pistol in there and cover me with it just in case," he told her.

Catherine did as she was told, and once she loaded the clip into the gun like her father had taught her, she aimed it at the door, ready to pump a bullet into anything that barged through it. She was a decent shot, but she had never shot a living thing before and she could only hope she was brave enough to do it if the need arose.

"Here we go," Weston said. He unlocked the door and peered through the opening and was very surprised to see who it was.

"Blake? What the hell are you doing here?" Weston said as he flung the door open to reveal a balding and very naked man. Blake stumbled inside; he was shivering from the cold and his feet were covered in mud.

Catherine advanced on Blake while keeping her gun steady. "Who are you and what are you doing here?" she demanded.

The man looked toward her but not where she was standing, as though he was blind. Weston closed the door and locked it to then walk over to Blake.

"Catherine, it's okay. This is Blake. He's my boss at the book store. We can trust him."

"Trust him?" Catherine mimicked. "He arrived naked in the middle of the night and you're telling me to trust him? How the hell did he even know we were here? Did you tell him?"

"No, I didn't tell him."

"Please help me," Blake begged, falling to his knees. "I don't know how I got here. The last thing I remember was lying down in my bed."

Catherine narrowed her eyes, still contemplating what actions to take against the naked man. Blake had obviously been sent by the Greys, but for what reason she couldn't fathom. He was unarmed and stripped of all clothing and dignity. If the Greys wanted to use him as a means to enter the cabin, it was a miserable failure because Blake was alone. She didn't relish the idea of having him stay in her cabin, but she also couldn't send him back outside, not if he was a friend of Weston's.

"All right, fine then," she said. "Give him some clothes to wear and we'll lock him up in the spare bedroom until we can work all this out."

"We can't lock him up," Weston explained. "I've known him for years. He wouldn't hurt me or you."

Catherine nearly screamed in frustration. "They sent him here, Weston! Do you think it was under good intentions? Just because we don't know how he got here doesn't mean it's safe to keep him here. For all we know, he's working with them!"

Weston avoided her gaze, silently agreeing with her. He put his arm around Blake like he was a wounded dog and led him down the hallway to the bedroom.

"Come on, Blake. Let's get you dressed and I'll put on a pot of coffee. Then we'll try and figure this mess out."

Catherine chewed on her fingernails, a nervous habit carried over from her childhood. She went to the front door and peered through the small window. Darkness greeted her and she stared into it, trying to make sense of the dark shadows.

The Greys were out there somewhere, she knew it; plotting and scheming their demise. It was only a matter of time before the dark figures came for her and Weston, unless Blake wasn't really who he said he was. Catherine recalled how the Greys were able to blend in as humans when they wore dark sunglasses, hats and clothing. What if they had chosen a different disguise this time? What if they could wear human skin, putting it on like a snug pair of pants and go unnoticed out in public. Or had they brainwashed Blake, somehow turning him into an unwilling pawn in their game of life and death?

She told herself she was being silly. If the Greys were capable of such a disguise, then why would they bother dressing up at all? Why wouldn't they just wear human skin and slowly integrate themselves into society instead of hiding behind long coats and sunglasses?

She slipped the gun back into the front of her pants, picked up the shotgun from where it was leaning against the wall, and headed to where Weston had taken Blake. As she passed an end table, she picked up a knife, one of three there, and slid it into her back pocket. *Just in case*, she told herself.

When she approached the bedroom, she found the door closed and locked.

"Weston?" She asked as she banged on the door and turned the knob.

He didn't answer. She pressed her ear to the door and heard a low humming, like that of an air conditioner.

Then Weston screamed.

His outcry jolted her away from the door. His scream was terrible, his voice filled with pain and unending torture.

She planted the bottom of her foot against the door knob, kicking with every ounce of strength she could muster. The door shook slightly and it took her three more tries before the wood cracked and began to splinter onto the carpet. On her fourth try, the door broke open. She took in the situation in the span of a heartbeat. It was an image out of a nightmare, horrors unnamed, and if she lived through the night, she knew it would haunt her for the remainder of her life.

* * *

A few minutes earlier.

Weston took a pair of pants and a shirt from a bureau drawer and handed them to Blake. He assumed the clothes had belonged to Catherine's father. As Blake dressed, Weston asked, "What are you doing out here, Blake?"

After dressing, Blake curled the thick blanket from the bed around his small frame. He hugged himself, as if the cold he felt wouldn't leave.

"I was getting ready to go to bed. I had just lain down and was going to read a book when a blue light shone through the window; it was like daylight. The next thing I knew I was in the woods completely naked. I walked for over a mile and then I found this cabin. What the hell is going on here, Weston? Is this something to do with that strange man who left that message for you? The one you had that meeting with?"

Weston sat down on the bed next to Blake.

"I have lots to tell you, half of it you won't believe but after what just happened to you I think what I say next won't sound so far fetched. I've seen it myself and even I still have trouble believing it.

But to answer your question, yes, there are these aliens called the Greys and they're involved. Catherine and I hope to stop them."

Laughter bellowed from Blake's throat. "Aliens, really? And you hope to stop them...you?" He continued laughing but it took on a different tone, like a recorder plunged into water.

"What's so funny, Blake?" Weston asked. He didn't take comfort in the sounds coming from the man and found himself wishing he had heeded Catherine's advice and hadn't let the man stay. But looking back, what else could he do to a friend in need?

"Whats so funny is how naïve you truly are, Weston. Do you honestly think an amateur video and a piece of 'Materia' will sway the general population? No one will believe you."

"Are you talking about the metal that bends like rubber? How did you know about that?" Weston asked, his hackles going up. His mind reeled with the possibility that Blake had been altered or was somehow being controlled. Then he saw something in Blake's eyes which gave him the cold chills. This wasn't Blake he was speaking to, not by a long shot. Blake's eyes were green, but the man before him had blue eyes and as he watched, all traces of their original color disappeared to be replaced by an empty blackness.

"You're not Blake. Where is he? What have you done with him?" Weston demanded.

The bedroom door slammed closed on its own accord, as if a strong gust of wind had blown it closed.

Blake rose from the bed. The blanket dropped to the floor and his skin began to ripple as thin limbs poked out the sides. His fingers popped and elongated as long thin arms unfolded and broke through the pink flesh. Blake suddenly grew very tall, towering over Weston as an adult would to a child.

"No..." Weston gasped as he took a step backward. Realization struck him at full force as he watched Blake rip off his skin as though it were a rubber body suit. "How could you do this? You...monster," Weston whispered. He was too enthralled to move as Blake transformed into a Grey. The figure stood before him, strips of Blake's flesh hanging in patches along its lithe frame. The only feature of humanity left remaining was the face of Blake, which the Grey wore as a mask.

The uncontrollable fear Weston felt transformed into a burning rage at the sight of the Grey looking down at him. He balled his fists and advanced on the being.

The Grey tore off the human mask and tossed it to the floor, the skin landing with a wet slap. Two black orbs stared at Weston, and somehow, he could still hear that awful laughter penetrating his mind.

Not knowing how long his courage would last, Weston sent a strong right hook into the Grey's belly. He immediately withdrew his left fist but it was as though he'd punched a brick wall.

The Grey didn't wait for Weston to try again. It came at him with blinding speed and wrapped its elongated fingers around his head.

Weston fought to pry the fingers away but they were latched on like suckers from an octopus, and the more he struggled, the greater the hold. He closed his eyes as the Grey stared into him. He focused on making his mind a jumbled mess of images so the Grey had nothing to control. He thought of sandy beaches, endless oceans, mountains rising out of the sea, birds turning into zebras, elephants running in Africa, lions eating, his first kiss, the day he'd almost drowned in the community pool and his father had rescued him, sharks, the taste of a cheeseburger, and on and on, image after image.

"What do you think you are doing?" the Grey asked in his mind.

Weston sensed the tension in the being's voice and made the collage of images morph and flash, speeding up faster and faster until they were a whirlwind of sounds, sights, feelings, and tastes.

"Stop it!" the Grey demanded, its hold lessening on Weston.

Weston pulled memories of television shows and movies, shows like *The Twilight Zone* mixed in with screen shots of *Gilligan's Island* and *Lost in Space*.

The Grey released its long fingers and broke the mind link.

"You're not so tough," Weston jeered as he slumped to his knees.

A flash of steel slipped into the Grey's hand. Weston didn't know where the knife had come from and he didn't care, he just wanted to get out of the room. He made his way to the door, trampling on pieces of Blake's flesh as he crossed the room.

The Grey attacked him before he was halfway across the room. A white hot pain lanced across his shoulders blades, peeling skin and muscle away in one stroke.

Weston screamed long and loud as white hot fire lanced his back. He tumbled to the bedroom floor. Blood seeped down his backside, drenching his shirt and staining the carpet a dark red.

The Grey hovered over him, a skeletal-thin giant wielding the blade which would end his life. Weston whimpered in pain as he raised his hands in terror, knowing he had seconds left to live.

"And now, you will join the others in assimilation," the Grey said, siphoning the fear from Weston and relishing his emotions. The knife lifted and bore down on his temple.

Two things happened what should have been the final moments of Weston's life. The door splintered open, sending splinters of wood flying into the air, and a loud blast roared over Weston's head.

The Grey was thrown against the wall with a gaping hole in its chest. There was no blood or ragged hunks of bones poking out of the wound though, the Grey was nothing but an empty shell.

Catherine shouted something as she stormed into the room, the shotgun blazing again, but Weston couldn't hear her. He couldn't hear much of anything after the first shotgun blast, except for a high–pitched ringing in his ears.

The Grey slumped off the wall like a wet dishrag and fell face down on the bed.

Catherine pressed the shotgun to its oval head and prepared to squeeze the trigger.

"Wait, Catherine," he said, his voice much louder than he intended. "I want to do it." He pushed past Catherine and rolled the Grey onto its back. Large black eyes stared up at the ceiling in defeat, the Grey was dead. Weston gazed into those dark eyes, then pressed his thumbs against the black orbs, and applied pressure.

The eyes caved in, revealing hard metal and a mesh of living tissue.

"What the hell?" Catherine said, puzzled, too stunned to move.

"It's some kind of metal but it's also organic," Weston stated.

"How did you know?" she asked.

"I figured it out after you shot it and there was no blood. There was nothing but a hole."

Without warning, the lights went out in the bedroom, plunging them into darkness.

"What the hell?" she said as she spun around to face the closest window. Through the trees, she could see a blue light was headed their way, growing in size, and pulsating like a heartbeat. "They're coming for us," she said.

Weston left the dead Grey on the bed, picked up the dead Grey's knife from the floor, and ran out of the room, bumping his shoulder on the doorframe in the darkness. "Come on. Let's give them a warm welcome." As he ran, he felt the blood on his shoulders. Reaching back, he touched it with his fingers and was relieved to see the wound wasn't as deep as he had first thought. But as soon as he could, it would need to be bandaged.

Catherine followed him, but her eyes were having trouble adjusting to the sudden darkness and she bumped into a wall.

"Hold on, Weston," she called after him, cursing under her breath as she rubbed her nose where she'd whacked it. She used her free hand to find the doorway and stumble into the hallway. Outside the bedroom, the interior of the cabin was bathed in blue light.

When she caught up to him, she handed him her pistol.

"Do you think that's wise?" Catherine asked, gesturing toward the knife. She hadn't seen him pry it from the dead Grey and didn't approve of it at all.

"We'll fight fire with fire," he replied. "Did you set the trap like you said you would?"

"Yes, it's all set. Something tries to get in that way they're in for a big surprise."

She moved close to him, standing beside him so close that their shoulders touched.

The back door rattled in its frame.

Weston and Catherine exchanged knowing glances as they waited in anticipation for the door to break open. A few seconds later and they got their wish.

Shortly after arriving at the cabin, Catherine had rigged the top of the door with a flammable mixture of gasoline siphoned from the car's gas tank and the four bottles of motor oil. When it has been blended together, she was confident she had a rough version of Napalm, the oil being the sticky part and the gas providing the accelerant.

When the door broke free, the oil spilled from the buckets to splash the Greys in the inky concoction, and no sooner were they covered, then Catherine sent a barrage of death by firing the shotgun.

The shot went wide but not so wide that the metal pellets sent up sparks, thus catching the oil and engulfing the attackers.

A horrible inhuman shriek deafened the night as smoke quickly filled the cabin. The strong odor of burning oil mixed with alien flesh stung Weston's nostrils and he fought down the urge to vomit, tasting bile in the back of his throat.

"Stay here!" Weston yelled to Catherine.

"No, I'm coming with you!" she yelled back. The inhuman cries had reached a crescendo and a few Greys ran off into the night, their bodies nothing but blazing torches.

Weston's frown took on long shadows in the blue light but when Catherine pumped the shotgun, reminding him of how she'd saved his life earlier, he realized she could take care of herself...and him if necessary.

"Okay," he consented. "But if things get bad I want you to grab that briefcase out of the closet and get out of here. One of us has got to live through this."

Tears formed in her eyes but she didn't cry. Weston pretended not to notice. He held the shimmering blade before him in one hand and the pistol in his other hand, as he headed for the burning back door. The orange light from the fire danced along the walls, the flames eager to consume the dry wood.

The acrid odor of the burning concoction caused him to cough and he had to cover his mouth with his sleeve.

"Be careful," Catherine said from behind him as she leveled her shotgun at the open doorway. One Grey was on the ground just outside the door. It was nothing but a blackened corpse, curled up into a fetal position from when it had died in utter agony. The others were gone, running off into the night.

He stuck his head out of the doorway, ducking back as the flames crackled and flowed like a living entity. The back door was hanging open and on fire, its hinges bent from the force of being kicked in. No Greys were in sight. But Weston knew they were out there, hidden in the darkness, just out of reach. Once they managed to douse the flames eating their flesh, they would return.

Catherine was still behind him and she looked down to see a handgun lying in the flames. One of the Greys had brought it, and as she watched the metal of the gun glow from the heat, she realized they were in danger.

"Weston, the bullets in that gun! Back up, don't go any further!" she yelled as she pulled him back inside the cabin.

"What bullets?"

As though on cue, a loud report filled the air and a cook-off round from the heated gun exploded from the clip and slammed into the wood near Weston's head, missing him by only a few inches.

"Jesus!" he yelled as he jumped back, more rounds cooking off to shoot into the night.

Catherine was now in the lead and she led them into the kitchen just as another blast sounded as more bullets in the clip ignited in the fire. Weston's ears were still ringing from the first shotgun blast back in the bedroom, but he could hear the bullets sing as they cooked off at random.

Once the explosions of the ammunition came to an end, they returned to the main room to defend the cabin. He didn't think the bullets had found a target outside—that would be too lucky for them—but they must've made their attackers hesitate for a few moments.

Banging on the front door filled the cabin and the couple swung to face the door.

Catherine leveled the shotgun and fired. Buckshot turned the midsection of the door into Swiss cheese and Weston clamped his hand on her shoulder to prevent her from firing again. She shrugged him off and crept to the door, filled with confidence thanks to the shotgun in her hands.

Lowering herself closer to the floor, Catherine looked through the holes—some as big as a human fist—she'd made in the door to peer out into the night. The air was cleaner near the floor and she sucked in a breath of air. Soon, she and Weston would have no choice but to abandon the cabin as the fire was now out of control and there would be no way to put it out. Behind her, Weston was covering his nose and mouth with his sleeve as he blinked through the smoke.

"I think I got another one," she said, as she looked through the jagged holes in the wood.

Before Weston could respond, two long hands shot through the door and wrapped around her head pulling her into the door.

"Catherine!" Weston screamed as he ran to her aid, but he was too late. More hands darted through the holes, snapping wood, and grappling Catherine's head.

"Weston, help me!" she cried as the door was forced open and she was yanked through the opening. Her scream was one, long single note as the Greys snatched her from the cabin and ran off into the night.

CHAPTER NINETEEN

Weston's first reaction to Catherine's abduction was to chase after her. He charged out of the cabin and into the darkness, heedless for his own safety, but the woods were silent and offered nothing to her whereabouts; it was as though the night itself had swallowed her whole, leaving no trace. He searched the sky for the blue light, but could only see a handful of twinkling stars. To the side of the cabin, there was an ornate glow as the structure continued to burn.

"Dammit," he growled in frustration. There was no trail to follow, no clue as to where the Greys had taken her, and no hope to save her.

Despite his anger and feelings of loss, he went back inside the cabin to retrieve a flashlight and whatever else he could salvage before it burned to the ground. He found a heavy duty Mag-light in the bottom kitchen drawer and after shoving it into his back pocket, he made sure to grab the keys to the car, then, after grabbing more ammunition for the pistol, he headed outside again.

Sucking in fresh air, he wiped his eyes clear of soot as he turned around to look at the cabin. The entire rear wall was now aflame as the tongues of fire licked at the night sky. Soon, the entire cabin would be burning. He turned his back on it, barely caring. All that mattered was to find Catherine.

At first he walked, checking for signs of a struggle near the driveway. When he found none, he quickly backtracked, heading into the forest. He stayed close to the tree line and searched for broken branches which might mark Catherine and her captor's passing.

As the minutes passed and he was beginning to become frantic with worry that he would find no trace of the Greys, he found what he was looking for. A section of broken and cracked branches, no bigger than three feet wide, parted as he pointed the flashlight at the tree line. Upon touching one of the broken branches where it had snapped, his finger came away moist from the moisture leaking out of the branch.

This was the path they had used to take Catherine, it had to be. It was fresh, no more than a few minutes old.

He walked through the opening, brushing his arms on the broken branches as he went. The wound in his shoulder flared up when a branch rubbed against it and he felt a small amount of wetness as the wound began to bleed. But he ignored it, moving deeper into the forest, the flashlight leading the way, his other hand holding the pistol before him.

Under the dense canopy of the trees, it quickly became darker and more ominous, the light from the burning cabin quickly swallowed up by the thick brush and overhead canopy of leaves. Twisted branches swayed in the chill wind, and tall trees took on the characteristics of the Greys. Every time Weston scanned the flashlight beam before him, he felt the night pressing in all sides not illuminated.

He soon lost the path he was following and began to travel in no particular direction. He attempted to listen for Catherine's voice but the ringing in his ears still hadn't abated and all but loud sounds couldn't be heard.

The shimmering knife in his back pocket began to vibrate and he paused, shoving the pistol into his waistband and pulling the knife free. He moved forward and the vibrations stopped. Curious, he took a few steps back and the knife began vibrating again. He moved west and the knife vibrated even more.

Grinning, Weston let the shimmering blade lead the way like a compass. Each time it ceased vibrating; he would search for the correct direction and then continue onward. The knife was homing in on something, but he didn't know what, though he prayed it would lead him to Catherine.

It wasn't until he spotted a pulsing blue light through the trees that he realized the knife had led him to a large craft, shaped like a giant triangle. It was in a wide glade and hovered a few feet off the ground. Swirls of mist came off the ship, blanketing the forest floor and Weston saw three tall shapes moving about in the blue light shrouded mist. All three were identical, with large black eyes, long fingers, and thin frames.

From where he watched, he was hidden from view, and he saw the figures had their attention focused on something lying on the forest floor.

It was Catherine.

Weston knew it was her immediately. He pictured himself charging into the mist and plunging the knife into one of them, then shooting the others in the head, but he knew that was foolish thinking. He couldn't handle one of them let alone three; they were too fast.

The knife continued to vibrate in his palm, threatening to jump from his hand, so he dropped it and didn't bother to retrieve it. He didn't need it anyway, he had the pistol.

He briefly thought of Blake and wondered if the real Blake had suffered much before he died. For now, the lasting memory of

Blake tearing off his skin and revealing himself as one of the Greys etched itself into his memory.

But that wasn't Blake. He reminded himself. *That monster killed Blake and wore his skin like a Halloween costume.* No, his friend was dead and had surely suffered greatly as he was skinned, no doubt, alive.

The image was still fresh in his mind and he couldn't help but squeeze the pistol in anger. The Greys had taken everything from him. His sense of security was lost. His sanity was pretty much gone, and now they had taken Catherine.

He wanted revenge and would get it by putting an end to them one way or another.

He moved closer, using the trees for cover. Each time he thought the Greys might spot him, he halted and waited for them to look the other way. He had nearly reached the clearing in the woods when he got a better look at Catherine. She was stripped of her clothing and lay on her back, staring up at the sky with a vacant expression. The Greys were moving all about her, examining her genitals and strapping a black device to her chest. Weston pointed the gun at the nearest Grey. The barrel swayed back and forth with the figure's movements, and it was moving too fast for him to get a decent head shot. Weston lowered the pistol. He was breathing hard, as hate and anger grew within him. He had to put an end to them, Catherine was depending on it.

One of the Greys knelt over her immobile body; it carried a silver cylindrical tube and scanned the object over her. From where Weston stood, he could see Catherine's skin begin to peel off. The Grey was taking her flesh, harvesting her skin so it could be used to infiltrate the human race. They were doing to her what they had done to Blake to get his skin.

Sudden, horrible shivers crawled along Weston's spine as he stared at the tableaux before him.

So this is the alien agenda, he realized.

The Grey moved the cylinder over Catherine's stomach and more flesh was sucked away. If she hadn't been paralyzed, not doubt she would have been screaming in agony.

Weston felt helpless and weak. What could he do for her? She was in the hands of beings from another world with superior technology. He could shoot them but what if he missed or worse, hit Catherine? As he contemplated the correct action to take, knowing he had only seconds to decide, more and more of Catherine's skin was being removed. She continued to stare into the dark skies above, seemingly distant from the terrible act being done to her body.

He couldn't let her die like this. He couldn't just watch her being systematically taken apart. It was time to act whether it was the right or wrong decision. He would kill them all or they would kill him, either way, he would do his best to save the woman he loved.

He stepped out of the trees and into the blue light streaming across the clearing. He stayed low, hunkering down in the rolling mist to avoid detection.

The Greys didn't notice him as they concentrated on Catherine. The flesh from her waist to the tips of her breasts was removed, revealing the red muscle tissue beneath. Oddly, there was no blood, as though the Greys had siphoned it off and were storing the liquid elsewhere.

When he approached from out of the mist, the first Grey to see him didn't stand a chance. The Grey stared at him, hesitating for one fleeting second, as if not believing someone had dared to approach, as if no human would have so much as attempted to stop them.

Weston used those seconds to his advantage and fired point blank between the Grey's oval eyes. He was a little off, though, and the bullet smacked the alien square in the center of the left eye, to then explode out the back of its head. The Grey toppled over, the odd-shaped skull shattering like glass.

The other two Greys were on him before he could so much as aim at them. They flanked him on both sides, expressionless and lightning fast. He felt a sharp pain slice across his right arm, then another along his right kneecap.

He knew what was happening to him. It was the same as last time, only this time the Watcher wasn't here to put him back together, this time he was on his own.

He started shooting at the blurry figures darting around him. He managed three unsuccessful shots before they disabled his gun arm. Then the ground hit his face as he realized they had knocked him down.

Long fingers tore off his jeans with such force it lifted him two feet into the air. Then his shirt was ripped from his back, followed by his underwear and sneakers. Now naked, he was dropped back to the ground, and he laid there, the dampness of the forest floor seeping into the wound on his back. He tried to scream, tried to yell for Catherine, but his mouth refused to work. He was paralyzed, like Catherine was, but he could still think, still feel.

Was this how Catherine was? Did she *feel* every second of her skin being flayed from her body?

The Greys began to fit a black device onto his chest similar to the one they had placed on Catherine's body. It wasn't like the one the Watcher had used to heal him; unknown to him, this one was the exact opposite. As soon as the device was attached to him, he began to feel his life-force being drained away.

Knowing they could read his thoughts, he started to form images of a large group of soldiers headed towards the glade. They were burly men, strong and thick skulled, their numbers increasing the closer they came to the clearing. All were armed with automatic weapons, grenades and flame throwers.

The Greys paused in their task to stare at him.

"You are lying, no one is coming here," one of the aliens said flatly.

"You're wrong," Weston replied back, using his mind, the telepathic link going both ways. "They were following me."

The craft hovering a few feet away shifted in color, going from a pulsating blue to a dark red.

They stared at Weston for another full ten seconds and it was all he could do not to crack and have them see through his facade. Then, the Greys turned and moved quickly to their craft, taking the black device from Weston's chest and scooping up the fallen Grey.

Weston didn't let up and produced more images of the soldiers getting closer and closer to the clearing, their hate and rage fueling them, driving them mad with bloodlust as they gripped their weapons with white knuckles. They would leave no trace of the aliens when they arrived; their orders were to wipe the area clean.

One Grey bent over Weston. He held the cylindrical device used on Catherine, planning on stripping him of his flesh.

"We cannot take the chance," another responded. "The Hive tells us this one has a piece of Materia hidden somewhere."

The other Grey was leaning over him, his head a few inches from Weston's face.

"Is this true? Do you have a piece of one of our ships? Answer me, human."

Weston tried to avoid the endless black orbs boring into him. He managed to turn his head slightly as he struggled to maintain the image of the approaching soldiers.

"Obey us. Do as we say," the Grey demanded, urging Weston with its mind.

The images of the soldiers faded and for an instant Weston lost control. It happened so fast that he barely noticed he'd lost the battle. The briefcase in the closet of the burning cabin flashed briefly and then was replaced by the soldiers. The armed men were closing in, witnessing the blue light and questioning what it was they were seeing but knowing they were headed in the right direction.

"Life forms detected," one of the Greys announced.

They pulled away from him and stood together near the hovering craft. Each one looked identical—a thinking, breathing entity.

A yellow light shot out of the craft and encased the three Greys. As the light grew in intensity, Weston had to close his eyes or risk becoming blind. Then, like a light switch turned off, the yellow light vanished, leaving only the blue mist to swirl across the ground.

Weston could feel something pulsing beneath him as the very earth began to vibrate, and a high whine came from the craft. Slowly, the blue light vanished, and as if the craft had been building thrust, it shot straight upward, disappearing into the night and taking its place among the stars; just another spot of light among millions of others.

As the craft disappeared, he found he was free to move and he rolled onto his side, fighting the bout of nausea filling him.

"Catherine?" he called. The sound of her name leaving his lips was cracked and lost. He rolled onto his belly and crawled over to her on his hands and knees.

Her eyes were wide open. She stared at Weston as he approached, as if he were intent on causing her harm. In her eyes he saw pain, intense pain he could only imagine. Large pieces of her skin were missing and she resembled a burn patient.

"Catherine, it's me," Weston soothed. He took her hand gently. "What have they done to you?"

She tried to speak but only a scream left her lips as whatever had held her paralyzed dissipated. She looked down to see that below her breasts to her waist, there was nothing but raw and red muscle.

A branch snapped behind him and Weston spun around in time to see a group of at least ten men carrying rifles gazing down on them. In the dark, Weston couldn't make out their features. The closest one was tall and burly, wearing a heavy wool coat.

A bright light pierced Weston's eyes and he held up his hand to block the light.

"Sammy," the tall man grunted to another man. "Turn off that damn light."

The flashlight paused over Catherine's body, and the men muttered among themselves, more than one of them crossing himself in fear. One man threw up, splashing the ground with his lunch.

"I said turn that fucking light off, now," the tall man snapped.

The light died and the men were once again lost in the darkness.

"Mister, why the hell are you naked and what happened to that woman?"

"You wouldn't believe me if I told you," Weston said. "Who are you people?" He was feeling weak, not believing that the images he'd conjured of an armed force coming to his aid had taken solid form.

"We saw a blue light in the woods and came to check it out. My name's Paul. We're on a hunting trip."

"Paul...a hunting trip..." Weston's voice went in and out.

"We need to get her to a hospital, pronto," Paul said as he pointed to Catherine. "Jesus Christ, look at her. Looks like a bear attack." He turned to another man. "Sammy, give that man some spare clothes and the rest of you get a litter built on the double so we can carry that poor woman out of here."

Mercifully, Catherine had fallen into unconsciousness, the pain of her torture to much for her to take. He took a pair of pants one of the hunters pulled from a rucksack and slid into them quickly. Then he leaned over Catherine, careful not to touch her wounds as he brushed her hair from her forehead.

"We're saved. These men are going to help us," he whispered to her. "It's all over, we won, honey, we made it." He turned to the men and pointed back the way he'd come. "Before we head to the hospital, there's a cabin about a half mile from here. It's on the way and her car is there. We can take that to the hospital."

"What's at this cabin that's so damn important?" Paul asked. His men were about finished with the litter and were getting ready to place Catherine on it.

A large, portly man came into view. He handed Weston a flannel shirt and a blanket. "Thank you," Weston said, not answering Paul's question but letting the activity of the moment make the man forget. Sure enough, a second later another man was talking to Paul and he had forgotten that he'd asked Weston anything.

Once they were dressed, the men picked Catherine up, gently placed her on the litter, and then draped her body with a blanket. Weston winced when he saw her face twitch and he knew that even though she was unconscious, she was in pain.

"All right, let's move out people," Paul ordered the men.

Weston grabbed Paul's arm and the tall man hesitated.

"You never said if you could take me back to the cabin. Can you?"

Paul nodded. "Yeah, it makes as much sense as anything else. Our cars and trucks are parked more than a mile from here so if yours is closer then let's go. You lead the way."

"Fair enough," Weston said and began walking while two men carried the litter with Catherine on it. Then he paused and jogged back to the clearing as Paul wondered where he was going. A moment later, Weston was back and in his hand he held the keys to Catherine's car. His old pants were ruined but the keys had still been in the pocket. He was also wearing his sneakers again which had been tossed away by the Greys when they had stripped him.

When they were halfway there, Paul caught up with Weston and asked him one more time. "You never answered my question back there, friend. What's so damn important at the cabin that it overrides your need to get your woman to the hospital?"

"Something that hopefully will at least make all the pain and suffering that both me and Catherine have dealt with worth it." Before Paul could ask him to elaborate further, Weston fell back to check on Catherine.

Deciding it wasn't worth pursuing, Paul said, "all right, men, lets move out and get this woman some help, quit fucking around and pick up the pace. This ain't no family hike we're on."

CHAPTER TWENTY

When Weston and the men arrived at the cabin, the charred remains illuminated the forest in orange and yellow streaks.

"Jesus, what happened here?" Paul asked as they approached the charred remains.

"Long story," Weston said as he reached into his pants pocket and pulled out the keys to Catherine's car. "Here, please get her inside and I'll be right there."

"What do you hope to find in all that rubble? Whatever you hope to find is nothing but ash by now," Paul said.

"Maybe, but if I'm right, then that won't be the case," Weston replied as he made his way to the burnt cabin. The area around the cabin hadn't burned thanks to the lush green growth and the open area between the cabin and surrounding tree line. He thanked whatever entity was looking out for him and Catherine for that. Things had been bad enough without being trapped in the woods with a forest fire raging at their backs.

He began to pick his way through the cabin. Some of the outer shell was still standing, but the interior was already nothing but ash and smoldering embers. He could feel the heat through the soles of his sneakers but he continued onward. He found the kitchen, the once white refrigerator now covered in black scorch marks and soot. From there he found the main room and where the closet would have been. Once there, he used the tip of his sneaker to kick some of the debris away. More than once his sneaker began to glow and burn and he had to force the tip into the ash to smother the embers. He was sweating now from the residual heat and he tried to cover his mouth as the ash floated all around him. Whether it was fate or luck, he found the remains of the briefcase. The case itself was burnt and destroyed and when he pried it open, the DVD was nothing but a melted pile of silver goop. But the piece of metal, the 'Materia', as the Grey had called it, was fine, looking no worse for wear after being in a raging inferno.

Weston bent over and picked it up, and though everything around the metal was still hot to the touch, the metal itself was room temperature.

He slid it into his pocket and headed back to Paul and the waiting men.

"Got what you were looking for?" Paul asked from the driver's seat of Catherine's car as Weston stepped out of the smoking debris. The engine was already running.

"Maybe, don't really know right now," Weston replied. His face was now covered in soot and he looked like an old time white actor playing a black man.

Paul waved for Weston to get into the passengers side of the car and he complied.

As the door slammed closed, Paul began to back up and spin the car around. "The rest of the guys are gonna walk back to the campsite and continue their hunting trip. I told them I'd meet up with them when I know you're all set at the hospital."

"Thank you, Paul, I don't know how to thank you for all this," Weston said. He winced in pain as he leaned back, his shoulder wound causing him some discomfort. It still leaked a little blood but for the most part had clotted, though the wound was filthy and dirt encrusted and would need a good cleaning at the hospital.

Paul waved the thanks away as he leaned out the window. "Think nothing of it, that's what we should do for each other, ya know, at least that's the way I look at things."

"How so?" Weston asked as he checked on Catherine in the back seat. She was still unconscious, but her head would twitch every now and then, as if she was having a bad dream. Her wounds were superficial, though downright nasty to look at, and he could only pray with proper medical attention that she would be fine.

Paul smiled. "Way I see it, we're all on this big blue rock together and if we don't look out for one another, then who will?"

Weston leaned back and let the cool air dry his perspiring brow. "That, Paul, is one of the most intelligent things I have heard in a long time."

* * *

Catherine stared out the window from her hospital room as dawn streaked through the seemingly impenetrable darkness. Her skin grafts were going nicely and in a few more weeks she would be well enough to leave.

"What's going to happen to us now, Weston? Where will we go when I get out of here?"

Weston had a few places in mind, but one stuck out among the rest. They had to move to a bigger city than Knoxville, Tennessee. A city which was crowded enough to hide them from the Greys and one that made it hard for the aliens to conduct a kidnapping if they ever tried for either of them again. He would take Catherine to a watchful city with eyes that never slept or blinked for that matter.

"We'll go to New York City and start over. Just the two of us," Weston explained.

Catherine took his hand and leaned her head against him.

"That sounds like a good plan," she mused, and nestled into his shoulder. She fell asleep within seconds and he gently laid her back onto her pillow.

With her asleep, he went and sat down in the only chair in the room. He picked up a magazine and crossed his legs, then began flipping through the pages. His back itched where his wound was healing nicely and he resisted the urge to scratch it. He thought back to the cabin and the silver melted goop that was the DVD. He wished he had time to make a copy of it after the Watcher had given it to him but there had been no time. If only the Watcher had been smart enough to copy it, then the evidence would have been so much more damning. But without the DVD, both Weston and Catherine had kept their mouths closed, saying they had been attacked by a bear in the woods after going for a walk. As for the cabin fire, a candle must have been left burning to then fall over on their walk and the place had caught fire. A terrible accident but there was certainly nothing sinister about it.

While he was reading, he felt a familiar vibration in his pants pocket. Reaching in, he pulled out the piece of Materia. He squeezed it, watching the metal bend and then reform. From time to time it would vibrate for no good reason and he had a feeling he could use the piece to find more of the Greys' ships wherever they were hiding across the planet.

But that was a story for another day. For now, he was content in knowing that Catherine would be fine and they would live a long and happy life together.

And sometimes, that's all one could ask for on this big blue rock known as planet Earth.

EPILOGUE

Richard Hart was an editor for the Knoxville Daily and for the hundredth time he looked at the manila envelope on his desk and what it had contained.

On the envelope in neat handwriting were the words:

View the DVD—The Watcher

In his twenty year long career, he had never seen anything like the DVD which came to him in the mail. If it was real, he was on the breaking point of a big story, and if it wasn't, he'd still have a story anyway. He saved the video to his hard drive and emailed it to a few of his friends and to the staff of the paper. One, Amelia, was a close friend since childhood, and she sent him an instant message with a link less than an hour after he had emailed the video to everyone.

Richard clicked the link and it brought him to *YouTube* where the video he'd just watched had already been uploaded, no doubt by one of his staff. If he found out which one, they would be looking for a new job.

The video was labeled ***Evidence of Alien Abductions*** and had a hundred thousand views so far.

Just as Richard hit the play button, there was a knock on his office door.

"Hold on a second," Richard replied. He minimized the screen and before he could call out, "Come in." Two men in black suits and dark sunglasses barged into his office. One was large and bald, the other blond and skinny.

"Are you Richard Hart?" asked the bald man.

"Yes, what's the meaning of this?"

He shoved him against the wall and handcuffed him to the water heater in the corner as the blond man began searching Richard's desk.

"Hey, you can't do this to me! Who the hell do you think you are?"

The blond man ignored him and quickly searched his desk. When he found the DVD, he took it.

"Who the hell do you think you are? You can't take that from me! You'll hear from my attorney!" Richard yelled. "Patty, get the police on the phone, Patty!" But his secretary wasn't answering him. "Where the hell is that woman?"

The bald man planted his meaty fist into Richard's stomach and the editor slumped over, wheezing. "If you know what's good for you," the bald man warned, "you'll forget we were ever here. If you want a reason then call it National Security."

"We got what we came for, now let's move out," the blond man said.

"Wait," the bald man said. He clicked the mouse, checking to see what Richard was looking at on his computer. The images on the DVD played on a continuous loop on *YouTube*. The world had been exposed and was now watching.

The bald man shuddered.

"What is it?" the blond man asked as he walked around the desk to see what his partner was so upset about.

"We're too late," the bald man said.

The two men stared at one another briefly before leaving the office and climbing into their black Sedan. Behind their eyes was one emotion that would gather and spread across the globe.

That emotion was the fear that we weren't alone.

DEAD RAGE

by Anthony Giangregorio
Book 2 in the Rage virus series!

An unknown virus spreads across the globe, turning ordinary people into bloodthirsty, ravenous killers.

Only a small percentage of the population is immune and soon become prey to the infected.

Amongst the infected comes a man, stricken by the virus, yet still retaining his grasp on reality. His need to destroy the *normals* becomes an obsession and he raises an army of killers to seek out and kill all who aren't *changed* like himself. A few survivors gather together on the outskirts of Chicago and find themselves running for their lives as the specter of death looms over all.

The Dead Rage virus will find you, no matter where you hide.

CHRISTMAS IS DEAD: A ZOMBIE ANTHOLOGY

Edited by Anthony Giangregorio

Twas the night before Christmas and all through the house, not a creature was stirring, not even a . . . zombie?

That's right; this anthology explores what would happen at Christmas time if there was a full blown zombie outbreak. Reanimated turkeys, zombie Santas, and demon reindeers that turn people into flesh-eating ghouls are just some of the tales you will find in this merry undead book. So curl up under the Christmas tree with a cup of hot chocolate, and as the fireplace crackles with warmth, get ready to have your heart filled with holiday cheer. But of course, then it will be ripped from your heaving chest and fed upon by blood-thirsty elves with a craving for human flesh! For you see, Christmas is Dead!

And you will never look at the holiday season the same way again.

BLOOD RAGE
(The Prequel to DEAD RAGE)

by Anthony Giangregorio

The madness descended before anyone knew what was happening. Perfectly normal people suddenly became rage-fueled killers, tearing and slicing their way across the city. Within hours, Chicago was a battlefield, the dead strewn in the streets like trash.

Stacy, Chad and a few others are just a few of the immune, unaffected by the virus but not to the violence surrounding them. The *changed* are ravenous, sweeping across Chicago and perhaps the world, destroying any *normals* they come across. Fire, slaughter, and blood rule the land, and the few survivors are now an endangered species.

This is the story of the first days of the Dead Rage virus and the brave souls who struggle to live just one more day.

When the smoke clears, and the *changed* have maimed and killed all who stand in their way, only the strong will remain.

The rest will be left to rot in the sun.

THE BOOK OF CANNIBALS
Edited by Anthony Giangregorio

Human meat . . . the ultimate taboo.

Deep down, in the dark recesses of your mind, can you honestly say you never wondered how it might taste?

Honestly, never wondered if a chunk of thigh tasted like chicken or pork?

Or if a hunk of an arm was similar to steak? And what kind of wine would be served with it, red or white?

Would a human liver be no different than one from a cow, or a pig?

For all we know, human flesh is as tender as veal, better than the finest tenderloin. And that is what the stories in this book are about, eating each other. But be warned, after reading these tales of mastication, you may just become a vegetarian, or at the very least, think twice before taking your first bite of that juicy steak at your local restaurant.

DEADFREEZE
by Anthony Giangregorio

THIS IS WHAT HELL WOULD BE LIKE IF IT FROZE OVER!

When an experimental serum for hypothermia goes horribly wrong, a small research station in the middle of Antarctica becomes overrun with an army of the frozen dead.

Now a small group of survivors must battle the arctic weather and a horde of frozen zombies as they make their way across the frozen plains of Antarctica to a neighboring research station.

What they don't realize is that they are being hunted by an entity whose sole reason for existing is vengeance; and it will find them wherever they run.

DEAD HOUSE: A ZOMBIE GHOST STORY
by Keith Adam Luethke

WELCOME TO DEAD HOUSE

The old mansion on the edge of town, aptly named Dead House, has a history of blood, pain, and death, but what Victor Leeds knows of this past only scratches the surface of the true horrors within.

But when his girlfriend is attacked by a shadowy figure one rainy night, he soon finds himself caught up in a world where the dead walk and ghostly wraiths abound.

And to make matters worse, a pair of serial killers are fulfilling carefully made plans, and when they are done, the small town of Stormville, New York will run red. The last ingredient to open the gates of Hell, and plunge this small upstate town into madness, is rain.

And in Stormville, it pours by the gallons.

DEAD MOURNING: A ZOMBIE HORROR STORY
by Anthony Giangregorio

Carl Jenkins was having a run of bad luck. Fresh out of jail, his probation tenuous, he'd lost every job he'd taken since being released. So now was his last chance, only one more job to prevent him from going back to prison. Assigned to work in a funeral home, he accidentally loses a shipment of embalming fluid. With nothing to lose, he substitutes it with a batch of chemicals from a nearby factory.

The results don't go as planned, though. While his screw-up goes unnoticed, his machinations revive the cadavers in the funeral home, unleashing an evil on the world that it has not seen before. Not wanting to become a snack for the rampaging dead, he flees the city, joining up with other survivors. An old, dilapidated zoo becomes their haven, while the dead wait outside the walls, hungry and patient.

But Carl is optimistic, after all, he's still alive, right? Perhaps his luck has changed and help will arrive to save them all?

Unfortunately, unknown to him and the other survivors, a serial killer has fallen into their group, trapped inside the zoo with them.

With the undead army clamoring outside the walls and a murderer within, it'll be a miracle if any of them live to see the next sunrise.

On second thought, maybe Carl would've been better off if he'd just gone back to jail.

ROAD KILL: A ZOMBIE TALE
by Anthony Giangregorio
ORDER UP!

In the summer of 2008, a rogue comet entered earth's orbit for 72 hours. During this time, a strange amber glow suffused the sky.

But something else happened; something in the comet's tail had an adverse affect on dead tissue and the result was the reanimation of every dead animal carcass on the planet.

A handful of survivors hole up in a diner in the backwoods of New Hampshire while the undead creatures of the night hunt for human prey.

There's a new blue plate special at DJ's Diner and Truck Stop, and it's you!

DEAD THINGS
by Anthony Giangregorio

Beneath the veil of reality we all know as truth, there is another world, one where creatures only seen in nightmares exist.

But what if these creatures do actually exist, and it is us that are only fleeting images, mere visions conjured up by some unknown being.

Werewolves, zombies, vampires, and other lost things that go bump in the night, inhabit the world of imagination and myth, but all will be found in this collection of tales.   But in this world, fiction becomes fact, and what lurks in the shadows is real. Beware the next time you sense you are being watched or catch movement in the corner of your eye, for though it may be nothing, it might just be your doom.

INCLUDES THE EXCLUSIVE DEADWATER STORY: DEAD GRAVE

THE DARK

by Anthony Giangregorio

DARKNESS FALLS

The darkness came without warning.

First New York, then the rest of United States, and then the world became enveloped in a perpetual night without end.

With no sunlight, eventually the planet will wither and die, bringing on a new Ice Age. But that isn't problem for the human race, for humanity will be dead long before that happens.

There is something in the dark, creatures only seen in nightmares, and they are on the prowl. Evolution has changed and man is no longer the dominant species. When we are children, we're told not to fear the dark, that what we believe to exist in the shadows is false.

Unfortunately, that is no longer true.

SOULEATER

by Anthony Giangregorio

Twenty years ago, Jason Lawson witnessed the brutal death of his father by something only seen in nightmares, something so horrible he'd blocked it from his mind.

Now twenty years later the creature is back, this time for his son.

Jason won't let that happen.

He'll travel to the demon's world, struggling every second to rescue his son from its clutches.

But what he doesn't know is that the portal will only be open for a finite time and if he doesn't return with his son before it closes, then he'll be trapped in the demon's dimension forever.

SEE HOW IT ALL BEGAN IN THE NEW DOUBLE-SIZED 460 PAGE SPECIAL EDITION!

DEADWATER: EXPANDED EDITION

by Anthony Giangregorio

Through a series of tragic mishaps, a small town's water supply is contaminated with a deadly bacterium that transforms the town's population into flesh eating ghouls.

Without warning, Henry Watson finds himself thrown into a living hell where the living dead walk and want nothing more than to feed on the living.

Now Henry's trying to escape the undead town before he becomes the next victim.

With the military on one side, shooting civilians on sight, and a horde of bloodthirsty zombies on the other, Henry must try to battle his way to freedom.

With a small group of survivors, including a beautiful secretary and a wise-cracking janitor to aid him, the ragtag group will do their best to stay alive and escape the city codenamed: **Deadwater**.

DEAD END: A ZOMBIE NOVEL
by Anthony Giangregorio
THE DEAD WALK!

Newspapers everywhere proclaim the dead have returned to feast on the living!

A small group of survivors hole up in a cellar, afraid to brave the masses of animated corpses, but when food runs out, they have no choice but to venture out into a world gone mad.

What they will discover, however, is that the fall of civilization has brought out the worst in their fellow man.

Cannibals, psychotic preachers and rapists are just some of the atrocities they must face.

In a world turned upside down, it is life that has hit a Dead End.

BOOK OF THE DEAD 2: NOT DEAD YET
A ZOMBIE ANTHOLOGY
Edited by Anthony Giangregorio

Out of the ashes of death and decay, comes the second volume filled with the walking dead.

In this tomb, there are only slow, shambling monstrosities that were once human.

No one knows why the dead walk; only that they do, and that they are hungry for human flesh.

But these aren't your neighbors, your co-workers, or your family.
Now they are the living dead, and they will tear your throat out at a moment's notice.

So be warned as you delve into the pages of this book; the dead will find you, no matter where you hide.

ANOTHER EXCITING ADVENTURE IN THE DEADWATER SERIES!
DEAD SALVATION
BOOK 9
by Anthony Giangregorio
HANGMAN'S NOOSE!

After one of the group is hurt, the need for transportation is solved by a roving cannie convoy. Attacking the camp, the companions save a man who invites them back to his home.

Cement City it's called and at first the group is welcomed with thanks for saving one of their own. But when a bar fight goes wrong, the companions find themselves awaiting the hangman's noose.

Their only salvation is a suicide mission into a raider camp to save captured townspeople.

Though the odds are long, it's a chance, and Henry knows in the land of the walking dead, sometimes a chance is all you can hope for.

In the world of the dead, life is a struggle, where the only victor is death.

INSIDE THE PERIMETER: SCAVENGERS OF THE DEAD
by Alan Spencer

In the middle of nowhere, the vestiges of an abandoned town are surrounded by inescapably high concrete barriers, permitting no trespass or escape. The town is dormant of human life, but rampant with the living dead, who choose not to eat flesh, but to instead continue their survival by cruder means.

Boyd Broman, a detective arrested and falsely imprisoned, has been transferred into the secret town. He is given an ultimatum: recapture Hayden Grubaugh, the cannibal serial killer, who has been banished to the town, in exchange for his freedom.

During Boyd's search, he discovers why the psychotic cannibal must really be captured and the sinister secrets the dead town holds.

With no chance of escape, Broman finds himself trapped among the ravenous, violent dead.

With the cannibal feeding on the animated cadavers and the undead searching for Boyd, he must fulfill his end of the deal before the rotting corpses turn him into an unwilling organ donor.

But Boyd wasn't told that no one gets out alive, that the town is a death sentence.

For there is no escape from *Inside the Perimeter*.

DEADFALL
by Anthony Giangregorio

It's Halloween in the small suburban town of Wakefield, Mass.

While parents take their children trick or treating and others throw costume parties, a swarm of meteorites enter the earth's atmosphere and crash to earth.

Inside are small parasitic worms, no larger than maggots.

The worms quickly infect the corpses at a local cemetery and so begins the rise of the undead.

The walking dead soon get the upper hand, with no one believing the truth. That the dead now walk.

Will a small group of survivors live through the zombie apocalypse?

Or will they, too, succumb to the Deadfall.

LOVE IS DEAD: A ZOMBIE ANTHOLOGY
Edited by Anthony Giangregorio
THE DEATH OF LOVE

Valentine's Day is a day when young love is fulfilled.

Where hopeful young men bring candy and flowers to their sweethearts, in hopes of a kiss...or perhaps more. But not in this anthology.

For you see, LOVE IS DEAD, and in this tome, the dead walk, wanting to feed on those same hearts that once pumped in chests, bursting with love.

So toss aside that heart-shaped box of candy and throw away those red roses, you won't need them any longer. Instead, strap on a handgun, or pick up a shotgun and defend yourself from the ravenous undead.

Because in a world where the dead walk, even love isn't safe.

ETERNAL NIGHT: A VAMPIRE ANTHOLOGY

Edited by Anthony Giangregorio

Blood, fangs, darkness and terror...these are the calling cards of the vampire mythos.

Inside this tome are stories that embrace vampire history but seek to introduce a new literary spin on this longstanding fictional monster. Follow a dark journey through cigarette-smoking creatures hunted by rogue angels, vampires that feed off of thoughts instead of blood, immortals presenting the fantastic in a local rock band, to a legendary monster on the far reaches of town.

Forget what you know about vampires; this anthology will destroy historical mythos and embrace incredible new twists on this celebrated, fictional character.

Welcome to a world of the undead, welcome to the world of Eternal Night.

BOOK OF THE DEAD
A ZOMBIE ANTHOLOGY VOL 1
ISBN 978-1-935458-25-8

Edited by Anthony Giangregorio

This is the most faithful, truest zombie anthology ever written, and we invite you along for the ride. Every single story in this book is filled with slack-jawed, eyes glazed, slow moving, shambling zombies set in a world where the dead have risen and only want to eat the flesh of the living. In these pages, the rules are sacrosanct. There is no deviation from what a zombie should be or how they came about. The Dead Walk.

There is no reason, though rumors and suppositions fill the radio and television stations. But the only thing that is fact is that the walking dead are here and they will not go away. So prepare yourself for the ultimate homage to the master of zombie legend. And remember... Aim for the head!

REVOLUTION OF THE DEAD
by Anthony Giangregorio
THE DEAD SHALL RISE AGAIN!

Five years ago, a deadly plague wiped out 97% of the world's population, America suffering tragically. Bodies were everywhere, far too many to bury or burn. But then, through a miracle of medical science, a way is found to reanimate the dead.

With the manpower of the United States depleted, and the remaining survivors not wanting to give up their internet and fast food restaurants, the undead are conscripted as slave labor.

Now they cut the grass, pick up the trash, and walk the dogs of the surviving humans.

But whether alive or dead, no race wants to be controlled, and sooner or later the dead will fight back, wanting the freedom they enjoyed in life.

The revolution has begun!

And when it's over, the dead will rule the land, and the remaining humans will become the slaves...or worse.

KINGDOM OF THE DEAD
by Anthony Giangregorio
THE DEAD HAVE RISEN!

In the dead city of Pittsburgh, two small enclaves struggle to survive, eking out an existence of hand to mouth.

But instead of working together, both groups battle for the last remaining fuel and supplies of a city filled with the living dead.

Six months after the initial outbreak, a lone helicopter arrives bearing two more survivors and a newborn baby. One enclave welcomes them, while the other schemes to steal their helicopter and escape the decaying city.

With no police, fire, or social services existing, the two will battle for dominance in the steel city of the walking dead. But when the dust settles, the question is: will the remaining humans be the winners, or the losers?

When the dead walk, the line between Heaven and Hell is so twisted and bent there is no line at all.

RISE OF THE DEAD
by Anthony Giangregorio
DEATH IS ONLY THE BEGINNING!

In less than forty-eight hours, more than half the globe was infected.
In another forty-eight, the rest would be enveloped.
The reason?
A science experiment gone horribly wrong which enabled the dead to walk, their flesh rotting on their bones even as they seek human prey.

Jeremy was an ordinary nineteen year old slacker. He partied too much and had done poorly in high school. After a night of drinking and drugs, he awoke to find the world a very different place from the one he'd left the night before.

The dead were walking and feeding on the living, and as Jeremy stepped out into a world gone mad, the dead spotting him alone and unarmed in the middle of the street, he had to wonder if he would live long enough to see his twentieth birthday.

THE CHRONICLES OF JACK PRIMUS
BOOK ONE
by Michael D. Griffiths

Beneath the world of normalcy we all live in lies another world, one where supernatural beings exist.

These creatures of the night hunt us; want to feed on our very souls, though only a few know of their existence.

One such man is Jack Primus, who accidentally pierces the veil between this world and the next. With no other choice if he wants to live, he finds himself on the run, hunted by beings called the Xemmoni, an ancient race that sees humans as nothing but cattle.   They want his soul, to feed on his very essence, and they will kill all who stand in their way.   But if they thought Jack would just lie down and accept his fate, they were sorely mistaken.

He didn't ask for this battle, but he knew he would fight them with everything at his disposal, for to lose is a fate worse than death.

He would win this war, and he would take down anyone who got in his way.

THE WAR AGAINST THEM: A ZOMBIE NOVEL
by Jose Alfredo Vazquez

Mankind wasn't prepared for the onslaught.

An ancient organism is reanimating the dead bodies of its victims, creating worldwide chaos and panic as the disease spreads to every corner of the globe. As governments struggle to contain the disease, courageous individuals across the planet learn what it truly means to make choices as they struggle to survive.

Geopolitics meet technology in a race to save mankind from the worst threat it has ever faced. Doctors, military and soldiers from all walks of life battle to find a cure. For the dead walk, and if not stopped, they will wipe out all life on Earth. Humanity is fighting a war they cannot win, for who can overcome Death itself? Man versus the walking dead with the winner ruling the planet. Welcome to *The War Against Them*.

DEADTOWN: A DEADWATER STORY
B OOK 8
by Anthony Giangregorio

The world is a very different place now. The dead walk the land and humans hide in small towns with walls of stone and debris for protection, constantly keeping the living dead at bay.

Social law is gone and right and wrong is defined by the size of your gun.

UNWELCOME VISITORS

Henry Watson and his band of warrior survivalists become guests in a fortified town in Michigan. But when the kidnapping of one of the companions goes bad and men die, the group finds themselves on the wrong side of the law, and a town out for blood.

Trapped in a hotel, surrounded on all sides, it will be up to Henry to save the day with a gamble that may not only take his life, but that of his friends as well.

In a dead world, when justice is not enough, there is always vengeance.

END OF DAYS: AN APOCALYPTIC ANTHOLOGY
VOLUMES 1 & 2
Edited by Anthony Giangregorio

Our world is a fragile place.

Meteors, famine, floods, nuclear war, solar flares, and hundreds of other calamities can plunge our small blue planet into turmoil in an instant.

What would you do if tomorrow the sun went super nova or the world was swallowed by water, submerging the world into the cold darkness of the ocean? This anthology explores some of those scenarios and plunges you into total annihilation.

But remember, it's only a book, and tomorrow will come as it always does. Or will it?

Blood of the Dead
A.P. Fuchs

Bits of the Dead
edited by
Keith Gouveia

Axiom-man
The Dead Land
A.P. Fuchs

$15.99
(Trade Paperback)
ISBN: 9780984261017

$15.99
(Trade Paperback)
ISBN: 9780984261024

$15.99
(Trade Paperback)
ISBN: 9780984261055
(Also Available in Hardcover)